THE LOVE RESET

NEUROSCIENCE TOOLS FOR SELF-LOVE & HAPPINESS

ELDIN HASA

My Daily Journal

Tools to positively change your life, self-love, happiness & improve relationships.

ENDORSEMENT:

"Life is about creating great, meaningful, and lasting relationships. Eldin Hasa has written a book to inspire you to have relationship mastery. Read, absorb, and create the relationships of your dreams and desires."

- Mark Victor Hansen, Author, Chicken Soup For The Soul

Best selling author of non-fiction books, sold over 500 million copies.

THE FIRST 100 BUYERS WILL RECEIVE A £100 NEUROSCIENCE COACHING SESSION FOR FREE FOR ONE MONTH!

I'm thrilled to offer an exclusive gift for the first 100 readers who purchase the book and leave a review on Amazon.

Here's how it works:
1. Leave a review on Amazon.
2. Take a screenshot: Capture your review along with proof of purchase.
3. **Upload:** Visit my website: https://www.eldinhasa.co.uk/the-love-reset-gift or scan a barcode below and upload the screenshot of review and proof of purchase.

In return, you'll receive one month of free group coaching, valued at £100 ($133)! This is my comprehensive 12-month group coaching programme, The Love Revolution - The Emotional Reset Blueprint: 12 Months to Your Best Self. Each week, we'll dive deep into transforming your emotional well-being and relationships, using neuroscience-backed tools to reset your mind and heart.

Remember, only buyers of the Hardcover version will gain access to the exclusive audio resources that are integral to your journey of healing, self-love, and emotional growth.

Don't miss out, be one of the first 100 and claim your spot in this transformative experience!

SCAN HERE

GET IN TOUCH:
eldin@eldinhasa.co.uk

BE A STOCKIST:
eldin@eldinhasa.co.uk

CREATED BY:
Eldin Hasa

Published by Eldin Hasa
ISBN: 9781399999939

**Copyright ©2024 by Eldin Hasa
All rights reserved.**

No part of this book may be reproduced, stored in a retrieval system, or transmitted in any form or by any means, electronic, mechanical, photocopying, recording, or otherwise, without the prior written permission of the author, except for brief quotations used in a review or critical analysis.

While the publisher has made a best effort in preparing this book, the author and publisher make no representations or warranties with respect to the accuracy, applicability, fitness, or completeness of the contents of this book. They disclaim any liability for any direct, indirect, incidental, or consequential damages arising from the use or application of the information contained in this book. The strategies and techniques described herein may not be suitable for every individual. The author and publisher are not responsible for any adverse effects or consequences resulting from the use or misuse of any suggestions or information contained in this book. The content is based on the author's thirty years research, experience, and opinions. If in doubt the reader should consult with a professional in the relevant field before relying on any of the information provided in this book.

First Edition: 2024

For more information about the author, visit eldinhasa.co.uk

DEDICATION

To my wife Nadia
&
son Sebastian

Free Resources

Scan a barcode to access
Free audio resources and
guided meditations

50% discount

Scan a barcode to access
50% off
The Love Rest 1-on-1
Neuroscience Coaching
Save £200

Contents :

Free Resources	6
About the Author	9
Breaking the Cycle of Toxic Relationships	13
Your Ultimate Magic Pill	15
Five Reasons You Will Love The Love Reset	17
A Guide for Everyone, Regardless of Relationship Status	19
How it works	21
Basic Principles	23
A Pathway to Profound Transformation	24
Why should I read and write as soon as I wake up?	26
Why should I read and write just before going to sleep?	28
The Solution	30
Accountability	32
Introduction	33
Swipe Right on Love	35
Chapter 1 Self-Love	37
Chapter 2 What is Love?	52
Chapter 3 After a Breakup	61
Chapter 4 Dysfunctional Relationship is Unhealthy	68
Chapter 5 Attracting Wrong People	78
Chapter 6 Dating with "Daddy Issues"	86
Chapter 7 Dating Apps & Mental Health	95
Chapter 8 The Path to True Love	103
Chapter 9 Attracting What We Are	112
Chapter 10 Giving & Contributing	121
Chapter 11 Happy Relationship	127
Chapter 12 Happy After The Honeymoon	133
Chapter 13 Busy After The Honeymoon	144
Chapter 14 My Other Half	148
Chapter 15 They Have To Make Me Happy	156

Contents :

Chapter 16 Myth 5: "As Soon as You Have Children, Romance Begins to Die"	164
Chapter 17 "Your Relationship with Yourself"	172
Chapter 18 Confidence vs. Desperation	180
Chapter 19 Joyful and Fulfilling Relationship	187
Chapter 20 Avoiding Convenience and Embracing Authenticity	192
Chapter 21 Myth Seven: Arguing All the Time is Normal	197
Chapter 22 Myth Seven part 2: Constant Fighting	202
Chapter 23 A Path to Lasting Relationship Bliss	207
Chapter 24 Breaking the Cycle of Conflict	212
Chapter 25 Creating a Magical Relationship	218
Chapter 26 The Art of Navigating Disagreements	224
Chapter 27 Respectful Communication	229
Chapter 28 Sustaining Love and Connection	234
Chapter 29 Injecting Fun and Humour into Your Relationship	239
Chapter 30 Never Stop Dating	245
Chapter 31 Sharing Life Lessons	250
Chapter 32 Emotional Support and Compliments	255
Chapter 33 Love, Intimacy, Romance, and Sex	261
Chapter 34 Sharing Goals and Dreams	268
Chapter 35 Compassion, Acceptance, and Forgiveness	274
Chapter 36 Mutual Desire to Step Outside the Box	280
Chapter 37 Admitting Mistakes and Communicating Effectively	286
Chapter 38 Discussing Taboo Topics	292
Chapter 39 Building a Relationship Foundation	301
A 90-Day Challenge	309
More About The Author	311

About the Author
How I Came Back from the Dead After an Adultery in 2009

Let me take you back to one of the darkest moments of my life in 2009. The pain of betrayal can break a person, and for me, it nearly did.
My world shattered in an instant when I discovered that my partner of many years had been having an affair, a five-year betrayal that shook me to my core. As if that wasn't enough, I soon learned that the two- year-old boy I had been raising, loving, and protecting wasn't biologically mine.

The emotional weight of the discovery was unbearable, and it spiralled me into a deep, dark place. My mind and heart were shattered, and to numb the overwhelming pain, I turned to alcohol. I started drinking heavily, bottles of wine during the day, several beers, and shots in the evening. This became my coping mechanism, and it didn't take long for the damage to catch up with me.

One day, it all came crashing down when I ended up in the hospital after suffering a heart attack. I was at the lowest point of my life, mentally, emotionally, and physically broken. Everything I believed to be true, every plan I had for the future, dissolved into nothingness. I couldn't see a way forward, I was contemplating suicide for many months, and began self harming. My mind was broken, and my heart was in pieces. It was as if the person I used to be ceased to exist.

But here's the thing about rock bottom, it's where you find out what you're really made of. When I was faced with this devastating reality, I had two choices: stay down or rebuild. I chose to heal.

The Journey to Healing
Healing wasn't a straight line. It was messy. I was angry, resentful, and lost. But I also knew that carrying this pain around would destroy me if I didn't deal with it. So, I started with my mind. I knew that before I could heal my heart, I had to rebuild my sense of self.

Here's how I did it:

Facing the Pain: I had to confront the hurt, the betrayal, and the overwhelming feelings of rejection. I realised that suppressing it only made it stronger, so I allowed myself to feel everything. Cry, scream, rage, whatever it took to purge the poison from my soul.

Reprogramming My Mind: Our minds are wired to replay the traumas over and over again. I knew I needed to break this cycle. I immersed myself in neuroscience, learning how the brain processes trauma and how to create new neural pathways. Daily meditations and affirmations became my ritual, rewiring my brain from a place of scarcity, fear, and betrayal to one of self-love, peace, and abundance.

Letting Go of What I Couldn't Control: The hardest part was accepting that there were things beyond my control, the affair, the deception, and even the fact that my son wasn't mine biologically. I had to let go of these things to move forward. Holding onto the hurt wasn't going to change the past.

Forgiveness: I realised that forgiveness wasn't for my partner—it was for me. Carrying anger and bitterness was like drinking poison, hoping it would harm someone else. Forgiveness doesn't mean forgetting, but it does mean freeing yourself from the chains of the past.

Rebuilding Trust in Myself: After a betrayal of this magnitude, it's hard to trust again. But what I found was that before I could trust anyone else, I needed to rebuild trust in myself. I had to trust my judgment, my strength, and my ability to move forward.

Rising from the Ashes
Slowly, day by day, I began to rebuild my life. I focused on the things that mattered most: my health, my mental wellbeing, and most importantly, my son. Though he wasn't biologically mine, he was still my child in every way that mattered. I poured my energy into being the best father I could be.

And through this process, I realised something powerful. Life doesn't break you, it breaks you open. It forces you to grow in ways you never imagined. That pain, that darkness, became the fertile soil in which I planted the seeds of my new life.

Now, years later, I look back at 2009 not as the year I died, but as the year I was reborn.

That chapter of my life, where I faced unimaginable pain, betrayal, and personal destruction, was not the end, but the catalyst for my transformation. I emerged stronger, more self-aware, and more compassionate. I realised that no matter how broken we feel, the power to heal and rebuild lies within us.

Today, I am not only healed, but thriving in ways I could never have imagined back then. I'm happily married to an incredible woman, Nadia, for 7 years, and we have a beautiful 3-year-old son who fills our lives with unconditional love and joy. Every day, I'm reminded that what I went through in 2009 was a blessing in disguise, a painful but necessary journey that shaped who I am today.

As a result, my life is now filled with health, happiness, business success, and purpose. My new book, The Love Reset, is launching on October 5th, 2024, where I dive deep into the neuroscience behind self-love, happiness, and rebuilding your life and relationships. I've built a successful coaching and consulting business based on neuroscience, and with my partner in the U.S., we've launched the Formula EQ Academy, where we train corporations and individuals on how to tap into their brain's true potential.

I also run a thriving property investment and development business, and have traveled the world speaking and teaching on stages about the power of healing, relationships, and the incredible capacity of our brain to create new neural pathways. I've written for top magazines, appeared on TV and radio, and have a U.S. book tour and multiple workshops scheduled for 2025.

My story isn't just about overcoming betrayal or heartbreak; it's about discovering the limitless power we have when we choose to heal, grow, and rebuild our lives with intention.

The journey wasn't easy, but the transformation has been nothing short of extraordinary.

And that's what I want to share with you all, there is always hope, there is always another chapter, and you have the power to write it.

If you're facing challenges that feel insurmountable, know that what seems like the end could very well be the beginning of the greatest chapter of your life.

If you're going through something similar, know this, you're not alone, and you will rise again. The human spirit is resilient, and you have the strength within you to heal, no matter how impossible it seems right now.

This is my story of coming back from the dead, and if I can do it, so can you.

Please reach out; You are not alone, I can help you as I have helped myself and thousands of people over the last 18 years.

I love you

Eldin Hasa

Healing Through the Hurt: Breaking the Cycle of Toxic Relationships

In 2009, after the betrayal and emotional devastation of an affair, I was far from healed when I jumped into the world of dating. Without fully addressing my inner wounds, I found myself in one dysfunctional relationship after another. Through dating apps and online platforms, I met women who were a mirror of my unhealed self. Yes, the hookup culture gave me momentary pleasure, but deep down, I was masking the pain of loneliness, resentment, and the belief that I was unworthy of true love.

I was angry and hurt, numbing the pain with alcohol and ignoring the unresolved childhood traumas that shaped my perception of love and relationships. I was a victim of domestic violence multiple times in three different relationships, each one more toxic than the last. I didn't realise that these cycles of dysfunction stemmed from the unresolved issues within me, issues that made me believe this kind of treatment was "normal."

It wasn't until I made a conscious decision to stop dating for a year, quit drinking, and embrace celibacy that I started to heal. I spent six months in India, living with monks and doing deep inner child work and trauma healing. That profound period of self-reflection and emotional work allowed me to heal on every level, mentally, emotionally, and spiritually.

Only after this transformation did I meet Nadia, my incredible wife.
Today, we have a beautiful 3-year-old son who fills my life with joy and unconditional love. Looking back, the pain and suffering I experienced were blessings in disguise. They were the necessary steps in my journey to self-love and true happiness. Without that journey, I wouldn't be who I am today, a man who understands that healing comes from within and that true love starts with self-love.

Those who don't believe in magic will never find it.
ROAL DAHL

Magic Pill

The Love Reset is your ultimate magic pill for transforming self-love, happiness and relationships, seamlessly blending cutting-edge neuroscience with actionable strategies to heal, grow, and nurture true love. It's not merely a book; it's a transformative guide that reveals how understanding the intricate workings of the brain and heart can unlock profound shifts in your love life. By embracing the magic within these pages, you will uncover how to overcome emotional barriers, attract fulfilling connections, and cultivate a love that continually evolves and flourishes.

Embrace the magic because this book offers a unique journey where science and wonder converge, creating lasting joy and deep, meaningful connections in your relationships. Believe in the extraordinary power of transformation, this book is your pathway to making that magic a reality.

"The Love Reset isn't just a book; it's a journey where neuroscience meets wonder, unlocking the secrets to transforming self-love and relationships into something truly magical."

"By understanding the intricate dance between the brain and heart, The Love Reset guides you to overcome emotional barriers and nurture a love that continuously evolves and flourishes."

5 reasons you will love The Love Reset

Five Reasons You Will Love The Love Reset

1. **Unlock the Power of Self-Love and Acceptance**
   Struggling to truly love yourself? The Love Reset helps you break free from conditional self-worth, guiding you to embrace unconditional love and acceptance of who you are.

2. **Break Free from Toxic Attachment Patterns**
   Tired of feeling stuck in unhealthy relationships? This book provides actionable strategies to overcome emotional dependency, helping you create fulfilling connections based on wholeness, not neediness.

3. **Stop the Cycle of Seeking External Validation**
   Do you constantly look for approval from others? Learn how to reset your mindset and reclaim your self-worth, so you can stop chasing validation and find peace within.

4. **Overcome Fear of Loneliness and Embrace Wholeness**
   Does being alone make you anxious? The Love Reset will show you how to find fulfilment in your own company, dissolving fear of loneliness and allowing you to thrive independently.

5. **Heal Emotional Wounds and Reclaim Your Inner Child**
   Carrying unresolved emotional trauma? Discover powerful techniques to heal past wounds, nurture your inner child, and rebuild your emotional resilience, transforming your approach to love and relationships.

The Love Reset is a powerful and invaluable resource because it offers a transformative approach to self-love, emotional healing, and relationships. By addressing deeply ingrained patterns like conditional self-worth, toxic attachment, and the need for external validation, it empowers individuals to break free from harmful cycles. Through practical tools for healing emotional wounds and nurturing the inner child, it fosters profound personal growth. This reset not only helps individuals achieve happiness within themselves but also enables them to build healthier, more fulfilling love lives based on wholeness and mutual respect.

Practical Tools and Exercises
Packed with actionable tools, exercises, and journaling prompts, *The Love Reset* offers practical steps to enhance your relationship. Each chapter includes exercises designed to help you implement neuroscience principles in your daily life. Whether you're looking to deepen your connection or overcome challenges, these tools provide a structured approach to achieving relationship bliss.
The practical exercises make it easy to apply the book's concepts to your own life, turning theoretical insights into tangible improvements in your relationship.

"Self-love is the foundation of any thriving relationship. Until you believe you deserve happiness, you will continue to chase it in others, never realising it's been within you all along."

A Guide for Everyone, Regardless of Relationship Status

Whether you're single, dating, or married, *The Love Reset* is designed for everyone. It offers valuable insights and guidance for improving any stage of a relationship. Whether you're looking to attract the right partner, enhance your current relationship, or heal from past experiences, the book provides relevant and actionable advice for every situation. Its universal applicability ensures that the book is useful for anyone interested in improving their self-love, happiness, and their love life, making it a powerful and invaluable resource.

"Embrace the magic within The Love Reset and discover how cutting-edge science and actionable strategies can turn your love life into a profound journey of growth and joy."

"The Love Reset reveals how blending neuroscience with practical wisdom can help you attract fulfilling connections and build relationships that are both deep and lasting."

"Greatness isn't born in moments of glory, but in the daily habits we choose."

How it works

The Love Reset functions as a daily ritual for your mind, heart, and emotional well-being, much like brushing your teeth is for your oral hygiene. Just as you wouldn't skip brushing your teeth, tending to your self-love, happiness, and emotional health through the principles in this book is essential for healing past traumas and fostering fulfilling relationships.

Each morning, as you begin your day, engage with the book's insights and exercises to clear away emotional residue and self-doubt. This practice helps you shift your mindset, aligning it with the love and happiness you deserve. Journaling plays a crucial role here, by keeping a dedicated notebook alongside the book's journaling pages, you can deepen your personal reflections, identify patterns, and track your progress towards emotional healing.

At night, revisit the lessons and prompts to process the day's experiences, reinforcing your journey towards trauma healing and self-love. This evening practice helps release any negative emotions, fostering peace and emotional clarity. Through daily journaling and introspection, you nurture not only your relationship with others but also the most important relationship, your relationship with yourself.

Just as maintaining good oral hygiene prevents decay, consistently practising self-reflection and journaling through The Love Reset will allow you to heal emotionally, grow in self-love, and build stronger, more fulfilling connections in your life.

"Morning reflections from The Love Reset set the tone for emotional clarity, while evening journaling fosters healing, turning trauma into personal growth and inner peace."

In today's fast-paced world, we're often bombarded with stress from work, discouraging news, and personal challenges that drain us. This book and journal tap into the transformative power of gratitude, helping you shift your focus back to the positive. Think of it as your mental safeguard against negative thought patterns, refreshing your mind and strengthening it against dissatisfaction. And as we heal and empower our minds, our bodies naturally follow suit.

Make this book a daily part of your routine to clear emotional blockages, foster meaningful connections, and continually improve your relationship dynamics. Consistency and commitment to this practice over the next twelve months will lead to profound and lasting transformations in your health, happiness and love life.

According to latest research from University College London, it takes an average of 66 days of consistent application to establish a new positive habit and make it automatic.

By integrating *The Love Reset* into your daily routine, you are engaging in a continuous process of emotional, mental and relational improvement, much like how regular brushing ensures oral hygiene.

Basic Principles

Both ancient wisdom and modern teachings emphasise the importance of starting and ending your day with intention. These moments are prime opportunities to reflect, evaluate, and set your direction. Yet, few people take advantage of this by establishing positive rituals that truly help them thrive.

Despite common beliefs, these rituals are not just for ultra-successful entrepreneurs or Buddhist monks, they are for anyone willing to take small, consistent steps toward personal growth. We recommend keeping this The Love Reset Book & Journal, by your bedside, with a pen within easy reach. Let it be the first thing you turn to in the morning and the last thing you engage with at night.

Spending just five minutes a day reading this book and journaling can help you create a positive mindset and actions that have a lasting impact. It's a small investment of time with the potential for life-changing rewards. Start today, and watch how your life transforms.

"Small, consistent steps lead to extraordinary transformations."

A Pathway to Profound Transformation

At the core of The Love Reset lies a transformative promise: to guide you through a journey of healing, rewiring your brain, and reprogramming your subconscious mind to create a life rooted in self-love, happiness, and fulfilling relationships. This book isn't just a reading experience, it's a daily practice designed to reshape your inner world and unlock your full potential.

Why this matters: By engaging with the tools and exercises in this book for 12 months, you'll systematically rewire your brain, build new, positive neural pathways, and elevate your self-love exponentially. This daily commitment helps break down deeply rooted self-limiting beliefs, heal emotional wounds, and free you from psychological trauma, giving you the foundation to thrive in all areas of life.

The Power of Consistency: Science and ancient wisdom both stress the importance of daily rituals. By starting and ending your day with intention, you can effectively harness the power of your subconscious mind. Consistent effort is key, these small, mindful actions compounded over time will create significant, long-lasting change.

How to apply the tools: We recommend keeping The Love Reset Book & Journal by your bedside, making it the first thing you turn to each morning and the last at night. Spending just five minutes a day with this book will help you cultivate a positive mindset and develop empowering habits. It's a simple, yet powerful way to reprogram your subconscious mind and set the stage for a more fulfilling life.

Make this a daily practice for the next 12 months, and watch how your brain, heart, and life transform. The journey is incremental, but the rewards will be life-changing. Start today, and see the magic unfold.

> *"Consistent, small, mindful actions compounded over time will create significant, long-lasting change, this is the power of daily rituals."*

"The early morning isn't just a time to wake up, it's a chance to align your mind, body, and goals before the rush of life begins."

Why should I read & write as soon as I wake up?

Have you ever had a day where everything just seemed to fall into place? Where life felt easy, and you could not help but smile? Imagine capturing a bit of that feeling every day.
"The Love Reset Book & Journal" is designed to help you do just that. In those first few minutes after waking, when your mind is still fresh, you have a unique opportunity to set the tone for the rest of your day. This journal prompts you with the right questions to build positive habits and start your day with intention.

Even if you are still groggy, take a moment to write in your journal. It's a small effort with the potential to make every day feel a little more like everything is going your way.

Feeling unmotivated? Write anyway.

Rushing out the door? Write anyway.

Growth is not always easy or comfortable. It does not come neatly packaged or wrapped in a bow. But the rewards of growth are priceless, leading to a thriving life, fulfilling relationships, and enhanced well-being.
Resistance can block the self-growth and relationship improvement you deserve. It can show up as depression, self-doubt, or bad habits like overeating or overspending.
However, by committing to reading this book and journaling each morning, you break through that resistance. You create an opportunity for positive transformation, allowing yourself to grow, strengthen your relationships, and move forward with confidence, leaving a meaningful impact on your life and the lives of those you love.

"Plant a seed in your subconscious before sleep, and watch it grow into clarity and insight by morning."

Why should I read & write just before going to sleep?

What do you usually do before going to sleep? Do you have a routine?

The average person spends over five hours a day watching TV, and if TV is not your thing, you are probably on your phone or streaming something online, often right before bed. But what if you used that time to invest in yourself and your well-being?

Writing in your journal before sleep is a step in the right direction. It is a small, positive habit that, when done consistently, can lead to spectacular results. Think about relationships: some are full of drama, while others grow deeper with time and rarely involve conflict.

The difference often comes down to small, consistent efforts.
Just as harmony in relationships is built through intentional actions, your well-being can be enhanced by dedicating a few moments each night to reflect and grow.
There is a little-known secret among couples who enjoy happy and fulfilling relationships. It contributes to their happiness and creates lasting bonds. The secret? They resolve conflicts before going to sleep, with love, honesty, and trust.
Similarly, writing in your journal before bed can transform your mindset. The Love Reset Book helps you shift your focus to the positive and disrupt negative thought patterns. Regardless of how your day went, reading this book, and journaling before sleep can improve your rest and overall well-being.
So, make it a habit to write in your journal each night. Even if you:
- Had a long day? Write anyway.
- Have a pounding headache? Write anyway.
- Have an early morning tomorrow? Write anyway.

Commit to this simple practice and watch how it enhances your life and your relationship.

"A person's strength is defined not by ease, but by how they rise when adversity strikes."

The Solution

Improvement isn't inevitable. Change is.
UNKNOWN

Congratulations! You have just committed to using this journal for five consecutive days.
It is commonly believed that if you push through resistance and consistently take action for a set number of days, it becomes a habit.

To give you a head start and help ensure this new habit sticks, here is a little motivation:

The Bad News: Research from 2010 shows that 88% of people who make New Year's resolutions fail to keep them.

The Good News: You're already ahead of the curve. You've taken more steps than most to stay on track.

The Better News: In the following pages, you'll find tips and strategies to help reinforce your commitment and make this habit stick for the long haul.

Consistency in studying this book and journaling daily for the next 12 months is essential because, according to neuroscience, it helps rewire your brain. Regular practice strengthens neural pathways, making positive habits more automatic. This consistent effort leverages neuroplasticity, allowing your brain to form new, beneficial connections. Additionally, daily journaling engages your brain's reward system, boosting motivation through dopamine release, while also improving emotional regulation and stress management.
Over time, this sustained practice leads to lasting change and personal growth.

"Growth begins when we honour the commitments we make to ourselves and others."

Accountability

CHOOSE A WAY TO KEEP YOURSELF ACCOUNTABLE FOR READING AND WRITING IN THIS JOURNAL

How to Stay Accountable with Your Journal

Maintaining consistency with your journaling is crucial for long-term success, and there are several ways to hold yourself accountable:

1. **Immerse Yourself:** Sign up for our curated email series at eldinhasa.co.uk. These emails are designed specifically for The Love Reset Book owners, offering daily tips, videos, and reminders to keep you on track.
2. **Buddy System:** Find a close friend or significant other who can check in with you daily, much like an accountability partner in a support group. This method is especially effective if the book was a gift, as it strengthens the bond and shared commitment.
3. **Visual Cues:** If you prefer pen and paper, use a calendar to mark off each day you complete your journal. This visual cue serves as a powerful reminder of your progress and dedication.

Accountability is crucial because, according to neuroscience, our brains are wired to seek consistency and reward. When we commit to a routine and have someone or something holding us accountable, our brain releases dopamine, a neurotransmitter associated with pleasure and motivation. This not only reinforces the habit but also makes it more enjoyable and easier to sustain over time.

Choose your preferred method of accountability, and let's begin this transformative journey.

"When you hold yourself accountable, you empower yourself to achieve greatness."

Introduction

In a world where love is often romanticised as something effortless, many of us find ourselves struggling to maintain the spark that once ignited our relationships. We enter into love with high hopes, dreams of a fairy tale romance, and the belief that our connection will naturally flourish. Yet, as time passes, the daily grind, unmet expectations, and unresolved conflicts can erode even the strongest bonds. The result? Relationships that were once filled with passion and joy may start to feel stagnant, strained, or disconnected.

This book is a guide for anyone seeking to create, sustain, and elevate a relationship that is not only loving and fulfilling but truly magical. Whether you are single and searching for your ideal partner, newly in love and eager to keep the honeymoon phase alive, or married and looking to rekindle the passion that first brought you together, this book offers practical wisdom and actionable steps to help you build the relationship of your dreams. At the heart of every thriving relationship is the desire to give and contribute unconditionally.

This book challenges the notion that love is something to be taken or possessed. Instead, it presents love as an active, ongoing practice, a commitment to giving, growing, and supporting your partner and yourself. Through this lens, love becomes not just a feeling, but a deliberate choice, one that requires effort, mindfulness, and a willingness to learn and evolve together.

Drawing on the latest insights from neuroscience, psychology, and relationship coaching, this book is designed to help you not only unlock the secrets to a deep and lasting relationship but also to heal past trauma, emotional wounds, and foster true happiness. Filled with journaling prompts, exercises, and practical advice, The Love Reset will guide you on a transformative journey toward personal and relational bliss. You will delve into essential areas such as self-love, communication, intimacy, conflict resolution, and how healing unresolved pain is key to unlocking the love and joy you seek. It emphasises continuous growth, happiness, and emotional resilience as cornerstones for a meaningful and thriving relationship.

One of the central themes of this book is that a truly magical relationship begins with self-love. When you learn to love and value yourself, you become capable of giving love abundantly to others. This inner transformation not only enhances your own well-being but also attracts partners who are equally committed to creating a healthy, balanced, and joyful relationship.

As you embark on this journey, you will discover that building a magical relationship is not about perfection, but about progress. It is about showing up every day with the intention to contribute positively, to understand and support your partner, and to nurture the love that binds you together. It is about embracing the challenges and triumphs of your relationship with compassion, acceptance, and a shared commitment to growth.

This book is not just a manual for love and healing; it is an invitation to transform your self-love and relationship into something truly extraordinary. By following the guidance within these pages, you will learn how to cultivate a relationship that is rich in love, intimacy, and connection, a relationship that continues to grow and flourish long after the honeymoon phase has passed. Welcome to the path of creating your own magical relationship. The journey begins here.

Swipe Right on Love, But Start With Yourself

Why Healing is the Key to Breaking Free from Toxic Cycles

In today's world of constant connection, smartphones, and dating apps, we are surrounded by endless opportunities for instant gratification. But this always-on digital culture often leads us away from the deeper emotional connections that build meaningful relationships. Fear of missing out (FOMO), the pressure to "keep up," and the lure of dating and hookup culture can leave us searching for everything but true love. Why? Because deep down, we are avoiding the most important relationship of all, the one with ourselves.

When we meet people through dating apps without healing our emotional wounds, we're stepping into a cycle of dysfunction. The unresolved baggage from past relationships, jealousy, mistrust, and feelings of inadequacy, follows us into new ones. Instead of finding love, we build attachments based on fear, insecurity, and control. The truth is, these dating platforms often become a mirror to our unhealed selves. We attract people who reflect the emotional state we carry inside, people who might be just as unhealed and emotionally wounded as we are.

Attachment, Not Love: Unhealed trauma drives us to form connections not based on love but on attachment. We cling to people out of fear, not out of genuine affection, and this insecurity manifests in toxic behaviours, jealousy, possessiveness, and the obsessive need to control. Constantly checking our partner's phone is a symptom of this deep-seated mistrust. Neuroscience shows that attachment arises from the brain's emotional centres that link fear and insecurity, while love is rooted in trust, vulnerability, and openness.

Repeating Dysfunctional Patterns: Unresolved emotional pain creates ingrained neural pathways that govern our behaviours. If we don't heal, our brains seek familiarity, even when that familiarity is harmful. This is why we often repeat the same dysfunctional relationship patterns with different people. The mind seeks to recreate what it knows, leading us to partners who mirror past traumas.

Jealousy and Control: Without healing, our insecurities dominate relationships, driving jealousy and control. We believe that controlling our partner will prevent abandonment, but this only fuels the toxic cycle. We project our fears onto our partner, while also attracting those with similar insecurities, deepening the dysfunction.

Domestic Violence and Trauma Transfer: Being unhealed makes us more vulnerable to abusive relationships. When we lack self-love, we unconsciously believe we deserve mistreatment. Worse, if children are born into these toxic dynamics, they inherit our emotional wounds. They witness and absorb these unhealthy patterns, and in turn, carry them forward into their own lives, perpetuating the cycle of trauma.

Breaking the Cycle Through Healing: The key to breaking free from this toxic cycle is profound healing and self-love. By addressing our childhood traumas, understanding our attachment styles, and cultivating self-worth, we rewire our brain to create healthier emotional connections. Healing reshapes the brain's neural pathways, allowing us to build relationships based on mutual respect, love, and trust, instead of fear and insecurity.

Ultimately, true transformation starts when we stop seeking validation or love externally, and instead, focus on nurturing love from within. Self-love is the foundation of every healthy relationship and the antidote to the dysfunction perpetuated by unresolved trauma. Healing is the journey that allows us to break the cycle and experience real, fulfilling love.

"True love can't be found through a screen, it begins when you heal the wounds within yourself."

"Repeating the same dysfunctional relationship patterns is your brain's way of seeking familiar pain, not love."

"Healing childhood trauma is the key to breaking free from toxic cycles and building lasting, healthy relationships"

Chapter 1
Self-Love

Self-Love as the Foundation of Relationships

"The best and most beautiful things in this world cannot be seen or even heard, but must be felt with the heart." This sentiment captures the essence of love and the deep emotional connections that define our relationships. The journey to finding love and building a meaningful relationship starts within.

The Importance of Self-Love: All the love you will ever need is already inside of you. The process of loving yourself is crucial, not only for personal fulfilment but also for attracting and sustaining a healthy relationship. When you love yourself, you no longer seek external validation. Instead, you exude confidence, which naturally attracts others who are also secure in themselves. This mutual self-assurance forms the foundation of a strong, balanced relationship.

Dysfunctional Relationships: Without self-love, relationships often become dysfunctional.
If you rely on someone else to make you feel loved and validated, you may attract a partner who is also insecure. This can lead to a relationship where both individuals constantly seek
proof of love and validation from the other, rather than giving love freely. The result is often conflict, unfulfilment, and eventually, a break-up.

The Inward Journey: The answers to everything you seek in love and relationships are
already within you. By cultivating self-love, you set the stage for a healthy, fulfilling relationship where both partners can give and receive love abundantly.

When we think about love, we often direct our thoughts outward, toward relationships, friendships, or family. But what if I told you the most important love you'll ever experience is the love you have for yourself?

Self-love is more than just a feel-good phrase; it's a practice that rewires the brain.
When we practice self-compassion and acceptance, we activate the brain's reward circuits, particularly in areas like the prefrontal cortex and ventral striatum. This not only enhances our emotional resilience but also fosters a healthier, more balanced relationship with others.

But here's the challenge: many of us struggle with barriers to self-love.
These often come in the form of negative self-talk, comparison to others, or past traumas that shape how we see ourselves. The good news? You can break these patterns!
The brain is neuroplastic, meaning it can change with practice. The more we engage in affirming thoughts and behaviours, the more we shift the neurological patterns that govern how we feel about ourselves.

So, how do you start?
- Acknowledge Your Worth: Daily affirmations may sound simple, but they activate key areas of your brain linked to self-worth and positive emotions.

- Practice Self-Compassion: When you catch yourself being harsh or critical, pause. Treat yourself as you would a close friend, with kindness and understanding.

- Be Present: Ground yourself in the present moment. A lot of negative self-judgment comes from ruminating about the past or worrying about the future. Practice mindfulness to reconnect with the present.

Remember, the relationship you have with yourself sets the tone for every other relationship
in your life. Tap into that unconditional self-love, and watch how your world shifts.

"When you practice self-love, you reshape your brain to function in a more balanced, harmonious way"

The Neuroscience of Self-Love: Why It's the Foundation of Healthy Relationships
Self-love goes beyond a feel-good concept; it's deeply rooted in how our brains function, regulate emotions, and connect with others. Neuroscience reveals that the way we love ourselves affects everything from emotional stability to the quality of our relationships. Understanding the neurological basis of self-love can shed light on why it is essential for building healthy, fulfilling connections with others.

Self-Love and Emotional Regulation: The Brain's Role
At the core of self-love is emotional regulation, a process controlled by the brain's prefrontal cortex. This region governs self-control, decision-making, and emotional responses. When we cultivate self-love, we enhance the brain's ability to manage stress and negative emotions, which are crucial for maintaining balance in our relationships. Those who practice self-compassion have better activation in the prefrontal cortex, which helps them respond to emotional challenges with resilience rather than becoming overwhelmed by fear or anxiety.
On the flip side, a lack of self-love often activates the amygdala, the brain's fear centre. This can lead to heightened stress responses, insecurity, and attachment issues in relationships. By nurturing self-love, you strengthen your brain's capacity for emotional regulation, reducing the likelihood of conflict-driven reactions in relationships.

The Dopamine System and the Pitfalls of External Validation
The brain's reward system, particularly the dopamine pathways, is responsible for feelings of pleasure and satisfaction. When we lack self-love, we become dependent on external validation, using other people's approval as a substitute for internal fulfilment. This dependence triggers the brain's reward system in a way similar to addiction, creating a constant craving for external validation. It results in a cycle where your emotional state is dictated by how others treat you.
In contrast, self-love activates intrinsic motivation and self-worth, generating feelings of fulfilment from within. This reduces the need to seek constant reassurance from others, allowing for more stable, mutually rewarding relationships. Instead of being driven by the fear of losing love, you engage in relationships from a place of security and inner peace.

Avoiding Toxic Relationships Through Self-Love
Without self-love, you're more likely to enter into dysfunctional relationships based on neediness or dependency. This occurs because the brain's fear centres, particularly the amygdala, activate when we feel incomplete or insecure. These emotions often push us into toxic relationships where both partners may use each other to fill emotional voids.

Neuroscience also explains that toxic attachments activate the brain's stress response, leading to an overproduction of cortisol, the stress hormone. This creates a state of chronic anxiety in relationships, leading to constant conflict and emotional turmoil. Self-love helps reduce this stress response, allowing you to form healthier attachments. It encourages a secure attachment style, where partners can support each other without becoming overly dependent.

Self-Love Enhances Empathy and Connection
The ability to love yourself also enhances your capacity for empathy, an essential component of any healthy relationship. Neuroscientific research shows that self-compassion increases activity in the brain's regions related to empathy and compassion for others, such as the insula and anterior cingulate cortex. This allows for a deeper emotional connection with others, as you're more capable of understanding and sharing in their emotions without feeling overwhelmed or threatened.

When you are at peace with yourself, you can offer love without expecting anything in return, and this creates space for genuine, unconditional love in relationships. It transforms relationships from being transactional, where love is given in exchange for validation, to being mutual, where love is shared from a place of abundance.

The Power of Self-Love to Rewire the Brain for Fulfilment
The journey to self-love can rewire the brain, promoting long-term emotional well-being. Through practices such as mindfulness, gratitude, and self-compassion, the brain's neuroplasticity allows for new, healthier neural pathways to form. This rewiring leads to improved self-esteem, emotional resilience, and a stronger sense of self-worth.

When you practice self-love, you reshape your brain to function in a more balanced, harmonious way.

This shift reduces stress, increases emotional regulation, and enhances the ability to experience joy and satisfaction independently of external factors. As a result, you become less prone to emotional highs and lows in relationships and more capable of sustaining lasting love.

Conclusion: Self-Love as the Key to Lasting Fulfilment
Self-love is the foundation of emotional health, resilience, and meaningful relationships. It regulates your brain's emotional responses, reduces dependence on external validation, and promotes healthier, more fulfilling connections. Self-love enables you to engage in relationships as a whole person, rather than as someone seeking completion from others.

By prioritising self-love, you cultivate a mindset and a brain that are capable of experiencing deeper, more authentic love, love that flows from a place of internal balance, emotional security, and true connection.

Journaling Prompts for Cultivating Self-Love and Building Healthy Relationships
These journaling prompts are designed to help you reflect on self-love, emotional healing, and the impact these have on your relationships. They aim to guide you through exploring your inner world and fostering emotional growth, based on the neuroscience principles discussed above.

Journaling Instructions:

- **Set aside uninterrupted time.** Find a quiet, comfortable space where you can focus without distractions. Try to journal for at least 10–15 minutes on each prompt.
- **Be honest and open.** The purpose of journaling is self-reflection. Write freely without judgment, letting your thoughts and feelings flow naturally. Remember, this is for you, so there are no right or wrong answers.
- **Revisit the prompts regularly.** Self-love and healing are ongoing processes. Use these prompts as part of your daily or weekly routine to track your progress and continue deepening your self-awareness.

Journaling Prompts:

- **Reflect on your relationship with yourself.**
  - "In what ways do I currently show love and care for myself? Where do I withhold love from myself?"
  - Explore how you nurture or neglect your emotional and psychological needs.
- **Explore your need for external validation.**
  - "Do I often seek validation from others to feel worthy or whole? How do I feel when I don't receive validation?"
  - Reflect on moments when you've depended on others to affirm your value and how that has affected your relationships and self-esteem.
- **Examine your emotional triggers.**
  - "When I feel rejected or criticised, what thoughts and feelings arise within me? How can I practice self-compassion in those moments?"
  - Delve into how your brain's fear response (amygdala) might be triggered and how practicing self-love can help you manage those emotions.
- **Visualise yourself as a complete person.**
  - "What does it look and feel like to live as someone who is whole and complete? How does this version of me interact with others?"
  - Imagine your ideal self, someone who does not rely on others for fulfilment. Visualise how this wholeness transforms your relationships.
- **Identify toxic relationship patterns.**
  - "What patterns in my past relationships have been driven by neediness or insecurity? How has this affected my happiness and sense of self?"
  - Look back at relationships where you sought emotional fulfilment from your partner and how it led to conflict or dissatisfaction.
- **Challenge your fear of being alone.**
  - "Does the idea of being alone trigger fear or discomfort in me? What are those fears, and how can I begin to let go of them?"
  - Confront any fear you have about solitude, reflecting on the idea that true emotional security comes from within, not from a partner.

- **Set intentions for self-love.**
  - "How can I incorporate more self-compassion and self-care into my daily life? What small steps can I take to reinforce my worthiness from within?"
  - Create an action plan to nurture yourself regularly, recognising how self-care practices enhance emotional regulation and inner peace.
- **Analyse your attachment style.**
  - "How do I typically attach to people in relationships? Do I lean toward secure attachment or anxious attachment? How does my level of self-love impact this?"
  - Reflect on your attachment style, understanding how your relationship with yourself influences your bonds with others.
- **Reframe your idea of love.**
  - "What would a relationship look like if it were built on two whole individuals coming together? How can I begin to shift my view of love from craving to mutual growth?"
  - Redefine love as a synergistic experience between two emotionally complete people, where love is shared rather than needed for fulfilment.
- **Cultivate resilience in solitude.**
  - "How can I practice embracing solitude and being okay with my own company? How can I find peace and fulfilment in myself?"
  - Consider ways to become more comfortable with solitude, learning to cherish your time alone and recognise it as an opportunity for growth.

Journaling Reflection:

After writing, take a few moments to review your responses. Notice any patterns in your thoughts or emotions that emerge. Are there recurring themes of insecurity, fear, or external dependence? Use these insights to identify areas where you can continue to grow in self-love and emotional independence.

Repeat this process as often as needed, and observe how your mindset shifts over time. By continuously engaging in this practice, you will deepen your understanding of yourself and strengthen your emotional well-being.

Journaling Prompts for Achieving Profound Self-Love

These journaling prompts are designed to help you explore and develop profound self-love. They will guide you in identifying the tools and practices that foster emotional healing and self-compassion, allowing you to build a more secure relationship with yourself.

Journaling Instructions:
1. **Create a calming environment.** Find a quiet, comfortable place where you can reflect deeply. Set aside 15–20 minutes for each prompt.
2. **Write freely without judgment.** Allow your thoughts and feelings to flow naturally. There's
no need to filter yourself, be as honest and open as possible.
3. **Be consistent in your practice.** Revisit these prompts regularly, as cultivating self-love is
an ongoing journey. Use this as part of your daily or weekly self-reflection routine.
4. **Review and reflect.** After journaling, take time to read over what you've written. This helps
you recognise patterns and areas where deeper work may be needed.

Journaling Prompts:

1. **Identify your current self-love practices.**
   - "What are the ways I currently show love, care, and kindness to myself? Are there areas of my life where I withhold love from myself?"

   Tool: Start by listing concrete self-love actions you already take, like self-care rituals or positive self-talk, and identify areas where you may need to give yourself more compassion.

2. **Release negative self-beliefs.**
   - "What negative beliefs do I hold about myself that prevent me from fully loving who I am? Where do these beliefs stem from, and how can I begin to release them?"

   Tool: Practice mindfulness by observing these beliefs without judgment. Begin using affirmations to challenge and replace them with positive truths about yourself.

3. **Explore self-compassion.**
    - "How do I react when I make a mistake or face failure? Do I show myself kindness or criticise myself harshly?"

    Tool: Develop a habit of self-compassion by using the three elements of self- compassion: mindfulness, common humanity (recognising that everyone struggles), and self-kindness. Write down how you can apply these elements in difficult moments.

4. **Visualise your ideal relationship with yourself.**
    - "What would my life look like if I fully accepted and loved myself as I am? How would I treat myself, and what boundaries would I set for my emotional well-being?"

    Tool: Use visualisation as a daily practice. Close your eyes and imagine yourself living in complete self-love, then journal the details of how this impacts your actions, choices, and relationships.

5. **Address your inner critic.**
    - "When do I hear my inner critic the loudest? What specific things does it say, and how can I respond with compassion instead of letting it dictate my feelings?"

    Tool: Practice reframing negative self-talk. When your inner critic appears, write down its words, then rewrite them as compassionate, supportive statements.

6. **Recognise external validation traps.**
    - "In what situations do I find myself seeking validation from others? How does this affect my self-worth and decision-making?"

    Tool: Work on internal validation. Each time you find yourself seeking approval from others, pause, and journal about how you can give that validation to yourself instead.

7. **Nurture emotional resilience.**
   - "How do I typically respond to emotional challenges or setbacks? What practices can I adopt to nurture emotional resilience and self-compassion during these times?"

   Tool: Develop a resilience toolkit. Journal about practical strategies (e.g., deep breathing, meditation, or positive reframing) that can help you cope with emotional stress while maintaining self-love.

8. **Reflect on boundaries.**
   - "Do I set healthy boundaries in my relationships, work, and personal life? How do these boundaries, or the lack of them, affect my sense of self-worth?"

   Tool: Use boundary-setting as an act of self-love. Write down areas where you need stronger boundaries, and plan how you can communicate them assertively and kindly.

"In learning to love yourself, you unlock the door to freedom, where your worth is no longer tied to anyone else's approval."

Alternative Journaling Prompts for Achieving Profound Self-Love

These alternative journaling prompts are designed to help you uncover deeper layers of self-awareness and healing. The focus is on building emotional resilience, self-compassion, and confidence through introspective practices that enhance your journey to self-love.

Journaling Instructions:
1. **Find a quiet space.** Ensure you have time to reflect without distractions. Creating a calming environment will help you connect more deeply with your thoughts.
2. **Write without editing.** Let your thoughts flow freely, without overthinking or censoring yourself. The goal is to express yourself authentically and openly.
3. **Consistency matters.** Set aside time regularly (daily, weekly, or whenever it feels needed) to work through these prompts. Self-love is a continuous practice.
4. **Reflect after each session.** Once you finish journaling, take a moment to review what you've written. Consider how the insights gained can influence your journey towards greater self-compassion and emotional healing.

Journaling Prompts:
1. **Uncover hidden self-judgments.**
    - *"What are the most common judgments I hold about myself? How do these judgments affect my self-esteem, and what would it look like if I chose to release them?"*
    Tool: Practice non-judgmental awareness.
    Write down the judgments you identify, then replace each one with an affirming, kind statement about yourself.
2. **Reclaim your inner child.**
    - *"What messages did I receive about my worth and value as a child? How do those early messages influence the way I love (or criticise) myself today?"*
    Tool: Use inner child work. Write a letter to your younger self, offering love, protection, and reassurance. Let this process guide you towards healing childhood wounds.
3. **Define your self-love rituals.**
    - *"What daily practices or habits bring me closer to self-love? How can I incorporate more meaningful rituals that nurture my well-being and emotional health?"*
    Tool: Design a self-love toolkit. Make a list of activities (e.g., meditation, gratitude journaling, mindful eating) that help you feel connected to yourself. Commit to practicing them regularly.

4. **Identify limiting beliefs about love.**
    - *"What beliefs do I hold about love and relationships that limit my capacity to love myself fully? How can I challenge these beliefs and replace them with empowering truths?"*
    Tool: Engage in belief-rewriting. Identify a limiting belief, then write a counter-narrative or affirmation that supports self-love and growth.
5. **Explore your emotional triggers.**
    - *"What situations or interactions trigger feelings of unworthiness or self-doubt? How can I respond to these triggers with compassion instead of criticism?"*
    Tool: Use emotional regulation techniques. Journal about how you can incorporate tools like deep breathing, grounding exercises, or mindful reflection when faced with these triggers.
6. **Examine your relationship with solitude.**
    - *"How do I feel about spending time alone? Do I avoid it, or do I embrace it as a chance to nurture my relationship with myself?"*
    Tool: Cultivate mindful solitude. Spend time alone each day, whether through nature walks, journaling, or quiet reflection, and note how this enhances your sense of self- love and self-awareness.
7. **Rewrite your personal narrative.**
    - *"What story do I tell myself about who I am? How does this story limit my potential for self-love, and what would my story look like if I wrote it from a place of love and acceptance?"*
    Tool: Practice narrative reframing. Write a new version of your life story, focusing on your strengths, growth, and the love you hold for yourself.
8. **Honour your boundaries.**
    - *"Where in my life do I need to set stronger boundaries? How do honouring my personal boundaries reflect my commitment to self-love?"*
    Tool: Use assertive boundary-setting. Write down the areas where you need clearer boundaries, and how you plan to establish and uphold them with confidence.

9. **Celebrate your uniqueness.**
    - *"What makes me unique and special? How can I celebrate these qualities, and how does acknowledging them strengthen my self-love?"*
    Tool: Create a self-celebration list. Write down your unique qualities, talents, and strengths. Reflect on how embracing these aspects of yourself fuels your self-love journey.

10. **Practice forgiveness for yourself.**
    - *"What mistakes or regrets am I holding onto that prevent me from fully loving myself? How can I practice self-forgiveness to release this weight?"*
    Tool: Use self-forgiveness exercises. Write a forgiveness letter to yourself, acknowledging your past and choosing to release guilt, blame, or shame.

Additional Tools for Self-Love:

- **Affirmations:** Create daily affirmations that challenge negative thoughts and reinforce your self-worth.
- **Mindfulness Meditation:** Regular meditation practices help you stay present with your emotions and increase self-compassion.
- **Gratitude Journaling:** Write down things you appreciate about yourself each day to cultivate a more positive self-view.
- **Mirror Work:** Spend time looking at yourself in the mirror and offering kind, loving words as a way of deepening your connection with yourself.

By using these prompts and tools consistently, you will not only foster profound self-love but also create a strong foundation for healing emotional wounds and building secure, meaningful relationships with others.

> *"When you love yourself deeply, you begin to attract people and experiences that mirror your own inner peace and joy."*

Chapter 1

Reflect on your relationship with yourself:
In what ways do I currently show love and care for myself? Where do I withhold love from myself?

Chapter 2

What is Love?

Love is often described as a powerful emotion, a deep feeling of affection, connection, or attraction to someone or something. However, to reduce love to just a feeling would be to underestimate its profound significance. Love is not merely an emotion that comes and goes; it is a fundamental state of being, a primary and default expression of the heart, and a core aspect of our human nature.

Love as a Primary State of Being
At its essence, love is more than an emotional response, it is a foundational state of existence. It is the intrinsic nature of our being, a state of wholeness and oneness that transcends individual experiences and emotions. This perspective views love as the underlying current of life, the force that unites all things, and the true essence of who we are as human beings.

Love Has No Opposites
A common misconception is that love has opposites, such as hate, fear, or indifference. However, when understood as a state of being, love is seen as a continuous, unbroken flow of energy that cannot be opposed. Emotions like hate or fear are not opposites of love but rather distortions or absences of it. They arise when we lose connection with our true nature, which is inherently loving. In the presence of love, these emotions dissolve, revealing the ever-present state of love beneath.

The State of Oneness and Wholeness
Love is often described as a state of oneness, a feeling of complete unity and connection with oneself, others, and the universe. When we are in a state of love, we experience a sense of wholeness, where all parts of our being are aligned and integrated. This state transcends the ego's sense of separation, allowing us to feel connected to everything around us.

In this state of oneness, love is not something we seek outside of ourselves; it is something we emanate from within. It is the natural expression of our true self, a state where we feel complete and at peace. This oneness is the reason why love feels so fulfilling and why it has the power to heal and transform us.

Reasons Why Love is Not Just a Feeling
1. **Love is an Innate Quality:** Love is embedded in the very fabric of our being. It is the essence of who we are, not just a fleeting emotion. This is why even in challenging situations, acts of love and kindness can arise naturally, reflecting our true nature.
2. **Love is Constant and Ever-Present:** Unlike emotions that can change from moment to moment, love as a state of being is constant. It is always present, even when we are not consciously aware of it. Love remains at the core of our existence, regardless of external circumstances.
3. **Love is Transformative:** When we experience love as a state of being, it has the power to transform our lives and relationships. It helps us transcend our fears, heal past wounds, and connect with others on a deeper, more meaningful level.
4. **Love is Inclusive and Expansive:** True love does not exclude; it embraces everything and everyone. It is an expansive state that unites rather than divides. In love, we see ourselves in others, and we recognise our shared humanity.

In summary, love is not just an emotion or a feeling that arises in certain situations; it is the fundamental state of being from which all other emotions flow. Love is the natural expression of our true nature, a state of oneness and wholeness that transcends the ego's illusions of separation. It has no opposites, for it is the all-encompassing force that unites us with ourselves, others, and the universe. When we live from this state of love, we align with our highest potential and experience the profound joy and fulfilment that comes from being in harmony with the essence of who we are.

To achieve and maintain an earth-shattering love that resonates through every cell of your being, it's essential to understand love not just as an emotional experience but as a fundamental state of existence. Here's a guide on how to cultivate and sustain this profound form of love:

1. Embrace Love as a Primary State of Being
Understand Love's True Essence:
- **Reflect on Love's Core Nature:** Acknowledge that love is not just a fleeting feeling but a foundational state of being. It represents wholeness and unity within yourself and with others. Recognise that love is your default mode of existence.

- **Meditate on Wholeness:** Engage in practices like meditation and mindfulness to connect with this intrinsic state of love. Visualise love as an energy flowing through every part of you, aligning your thoughts, emotions, and actions with this core essence.

2. Cultivate a Continuous Flow of Love
Practice Unconditional Love:
- **Develop Self-Love:** Begin with yourself. Cultivate self-love by treating yourself with kindness, compassion, and acceptance. Understand that you are deserving of love and that it is an innate part of who you are.
- **Extend Love to Others:** In your interactions, aim to give love without expecting anything in return. This will create a continuous flow of love that reinforces its presence in your life.

3. Transcend Opposites and Embrace Unity
Let Go of Negative Emotions:
- **Acknowledge and Release:** Understand that negative emotions such as fear or hate are distortions of love. Practice acknowledging these emotions without judgment and work on letting them dissolve by reconnecting with your core state of love.
- **Focus on Connection:** Shift your focus from conflict and separation to connection and unity. Engage in practices that enhance your sense of oneness with others, such as empathy exercises and active listening.

4. Foster a Sense of Oneness and Integration
Create Unity Within Yourself:
- **Integrate All Parts of Yourself:** Ensure that your actions, thoughts, and emotions are aligned with your sense of love. This can be achieved through practices like journaling, self-reflection, and setting intentional goals that align with your core values.
- **Experience Connection:** Engage in activities that foster a sense of unity with others and the world. Participate in group activities, community service, or spiritual practices that emphasise interconnectedness.

5. Embrace Love's Transformative and Expansive Nature
Allow Love to Transform Your Life:
- **Heal and Grow:** Use love as a tool for personal growth and healing. Address past wounds with compassion and work towards self-improvement in alignment with your loving nature.
- **Expand Your Horizons:** Recognise that love is inclusive and expansive. Embrace diversity in your relationships and experiences. Seek to understand and connect with others from different backgrounds and perspectives.

To live in a state of profound love that permeates every cell of your being, you must view love as your fundamental state of existence rather than a temporary feeling. By embracing love as a primary and continuous state, transcending negative emotions, fostering unity, and allowing love to transform and expand your life, you align with your true essence and experience the deep fulfilment and joy that come from living in harmony with love.

> *"When we live in love, we align with our highest potential, embracing the oneness that unites us all."*

Journaling Prompts

Here are three journaling prompts designed to help you explore and cultivate a deep, fundamental love that resonates through every aspect of your being:

1. Exploring Your Fundamental State of Love
Prompt: Reflect on a time when you felt a deep sense of wholeness and connection with yourself and others. How did this experience align with your understanding of love as a primary state of being? Describe how you felt and what aspects of this state you wish to cultivate more in your daily life.

Instructions:
- Spend a few minutes in a quiet space, thinking about this experience.
- Write freely about the feelings of unity and completeness you experienced.
- Identify specific actions or practices that helped you connect with this state and how you can integrate them into your current life.

2. Transcending Negative Emotions
Prompt: Consider a recent situation where you felt emotions like fear, anger, or sadness. How did these emotions affect your sense of love and connection? How can you reconnect with your fundamental state of love to address and transform these emotions?

Instructions:
- Reflect on the specific situation and emotions you felt.
- Journal about how these emotions diverged from your sense of love and connection.
- Write about practical steps you can take to re-align with your state of love, such as mindfulness, self-compassion, or seeking support.

3. Fostering Oneness and Integration

Prompt: Write about how you can create more unity within yourself and in your relationships. What are some ways you can align your actions, thoughts, and emotions with your sense of love? How can you enhance your sense of oneness with others and the world around you?

Instructions:
- Reflect on the aspects of your life where you feel a lack of unity or alignment.
- List specific actions or practices that can help you integrate and harmonise your sense of love with your daily life.
- Consider how you can extend this sense of oneness to your interactions with others and your broader community.

Journaling Instructions
1. **Set the Scene:** Find a quiet, comfortable space where you can write without interruptions. Take a few deep breaths to centre yourself before starting.
2. **Write Freely:** Allow yourself to write without self-censorship. Let your thoughts flow naturally as you respond to each prompt. Remember, there are no right or wrong answers—focus on exploring your feelings and insights.
3. **Reflect and Integrate:** After writing, take a moment to reflect on what you've written. Consider how these insights can be applied to your daily life to deepen your experience of love and connection.
4. **Regular Practice:** Make journaling a regular part of your routine to continuously explore and nurture your fundamental state of love. Aim to revisit these prompts periodically to track your growth and transformation.

Feel free to use several additional blank pages in your notebook, in addition to the ones provided in this book. These extra pages will allow you to dive deeper into the journaling prompts and exercises, giving you space to explore your thoughts and feelings more fully. Whether you're working through complex emotions, visualising your ideal relationship, or reflecting on past experiences, having extra space will give you the freedom to express yourself without limitations. Take your time, and let your reflections flow naturally.

By integrating these journaling practices into your daily routine, you'll develop a richer, more nuanced understanding of love as a state of being, ultimately fostering greater connection, wholeness, and fulfilment in your life and relationships.

"Love is the essence of who we are, an ever-present state of wholeness that transcends mere emotion."

"In love, we find our oneness and wholeness, where the illusion of separation dissolves into connection."

"Love has no opposites; it is the all-encompassing force that heals, transforms, and brings us into harmony with life."

Chapter 2

Understanding Love Beyond Emotion

Reflect on a time when you felt deeply connected to someone or something. How did this experience go beyond just a fleeting feeling? What did it reveal to you about the nature of love as a state of being?

Chapter 3
After a Breakup

The Heart's Role in Emotional Healing
After a breakup, it's not just the mind that suffers, your heart does too. The emotional pain we experience is often felt deeply in the heart, as it is directly connected to our emotional experiences through this intricate nervous system. The heart's "brain" plays a crucial role in processing emotions, and it communicates these feelings to the brain, which in turn affects how we think, behave, and even how we heal from emotional wounds.
Healing after a breakup, therefore, isn't just about mentally processing the experience, it's about addressing the emotional trauma stored in the heart. The heart's independent nervous system can hold onto pain, grief, and unresolved emotions, which can impact not only your emotional health but also your ability to form healthy relationships in the future.

The Science Behind the Heart's Power
The heart generates the strongest electromagnetic field in the body, much stronger than the brain's. This field is so powerful that it can be detected several feet away from the body, and it plays a significant role in attracting or repelling people and experiences into our lives. This is why maintaining elevated emotions such as love, gratitude, and compassion is essential for attracting positive experiences, including a healthy, loving partner.
When you experience negative emotions, such as fear or anger, this electromagnetic field becomes chaotic, reflecting the disarray within your emotional state. Conversely, when you cultivate positive emotions, your heart's electromagnetic field becomes coherent and harmonious, creating a powerful force that attracts positive experiences and relationships into your life.

The Importance of Healing the Heart
After a breakup, it's crucial to heal the heart before entering a new relationship. If the heart remains wounded, it can send negative signals to the brain, leading to repeated patterns of dysfunctional relationships.

The unresolved emotional trauma in the heart can cause you to attract partners who mirror your unhealed wounds, perpetuating a cycle of pain and disappointment.

Healing the heart involves addressing these emotional wounds, working through past traumas, and restoring coherence to the heart's electromagnetic field. Practices like mindfulness, meditation, and heart-focused breathing can help align your heart and mind, creating a state of inner harmony that is essential for attracting a truly magical relationship.

The Heart as a Gateway to a Magical Relationship
To achieve a truly magical relationship, you must first heal the function and structure of your heart's "brain." This healing process involves deep inner work, reflecting on past relationships, understanding your emotional triggers, and cultivating self-love and compassion. By doing this work, you clear the emotional blockages that may be preventing you from experiencing the love and connection you desire.

Only by becoming whole and healed can you attract a partner who is also whole and ready for a deep, meaningful connection. When your heart is healed and coherent, it acts as a powerful magnet, drawing in a partner who resonates with your elevated emotional state. Together, you can create a relationship that is not only fulfilling but truly extraordinary.

In summary, "The Love Reset" emphasises the essential role of the heart in both emotional healing and relationship-building. By understanding and harnessing the power of the heart, you can heal from past traumas, align your emotions with your desires, and attract the love you truly deserve.

Journaling Prompts

Here are journal prompts to help you heal your heart, harness its power, and prepare for a truly magical relationship:

1. Reflecting on Emotional Wounds
What past experiences or relationships have left emotional scars on your heart? How do these unresolved emotions manifest in your current thoughts, feelings, and actions?

This prompt encourages you to delve deep into the emotional wounds you have carried, which may still affect your current state of being. By identifying and acknowledging these scars, you begin the process of healing. Understanding the origin of your pain is the first step toward releasing it.

2. Understanding Heart-Brain Communication

How does your heart feel today? Take a moment to listen to your heart without judgment. What emotions are you holding onto, and how might these be influencing your thoughts and decisions?

This exercise helps you connect with the heart's intrinsic intelligence. By tuning into your heart's emotional state, you can begin to understand how it communicates with your brain, affecting your overall emotional and mental well-being. It is about cultivating a deep awareness of the heart's signals.

3. Cultivating Heart Coherence

When was the last time you felt true love, joy, or gratitude? Describe the experience in detail. How did your heart feel during this time? How can you bring more of these emotions into your daily life?

This prompt is designed to help you recall and amplify positive emotional experiences.

By focusing on moments of love, joy, and gratitude, you can cultivate heart coherence, a state where the heart's electromagnetic field becomes harmonious and powerful, positively influencing your life.

4. Healing After a Breakup

What are the most painful memories from your past relationships? How have these experiences shaped your beliefs about love and partnership? What do you need to release in order to heal?

After a breakup, it's crucial to address the pain that lingers in the heart. This prompt encourages you to confront the painful memories and the limiting beliefs they've created. By articulating these feelings, you can begin the process of letting go and making space for new, healthier beliefs about love.

5. Exploring the Heart's Electromagnetic Influence

Consider the energy you emit when you're around others. How do you think your current emotional state affects the people and situations you attract? What changes can you make to align your heart's energy with the kind of relationship you desire?

This prompt focuses on the heart's electromagnetic field and how it influences your interactions and relationships. By becoming aware of the energy you are putting out into the world, you can make conscious efforts to shift it toward positivity, thereby attracting more harmonious relationships.

6. Creating a Vision of Love
Visualise your ideal relationship. What does it feel like? How do you and your partner communicate, support each other, and grow together? Write down this vision in as much detail as possible.

Visualisation is a powerful tool for manifesting the future you desire. This prompt guides you in creating a vivid picture of your ideal relationship, helping you to align your heart and mind with the reality you want to attract.

7. Developing Self-Love
What does self-love mean to you? In what ways have you nurtured or neglected your own heart? How can you start showing yourself more love and compassion?

Before you can attract a loving partner, it's essential to cultivate self-love. This prompt encourages introspection on how you treat yourself and offers a pathway to develop a deeper, more compassionate relationship with your own heart.

8. Releasing Limiting Beliefs
Prompt: What negative beliefs about love and relationships do you hold? Where did these beliefs originate, and how have they impacted your past relationships? What new beliefs would better serve your journey to a healthy relationship?

Limiting beliefs can create significant barriers to love. This prompt helps you identify and challenge these beliefs, replacing them with more empowering thoughts that support your goal of attracting a fulfilling relationship.

9. Aligning with Your Heart's Desires
What does your heart truly desire in a relationship? How can you align your actions and decisions with these desires to attract the partner and love you seek?

This prompt encourages you to clarify your true desires, which may be buried beneath fear or past pain. Aligning your actions with these desires will help you move closer to the relationship you want to manifest.

10. Daily Heart-Centred Practices

What daily practices can you incorporate to maintain heart coherence and emotional well-being? How will you commit to these practices, and what benefits do you expect to see in your life and relationships?

Consistent daily practices, such as meditation, gratitude journaling, or heart-focused breathing, are essential for maintaining the health and coherence of your heart.

This prompt helps you design a routine that supports ongoing emotional and relational growth.

These journal prompts guide you through a deep exploration of the heart's power and the healing process necessary to create the love life you desire. By regularly engaging with these prompts, you can heal old wounds, cultivate self-love, and align your heart's energy to attract the kind of relationship you truly want.

Journaling Instructions

On the following pages, take the time to answer the questions from the journaling prompts provided in this chapter. These prompts are designed to help you reflect deeply on yourself and relationship, uncover new insights, and foster greater understanding.

Feel free to take as many extra blank pages as you need for your responses. There's no right or wrong way to journal, what is important is that you engage with the prompts honestly and consistently.

Frequent journaling using these prompts can lead to exponential improvements in yourself, your relationship, helping you to build a deeper, more meaningful connection with your partner.

Feel free to use several additional blank pages in your notebook, in addition to the ones provided in this book. These extra pages will allow you to dive deeper into the journaling prompts and exercises, giving you space to explore your thoughts and feelings more fully. Whether you're working through complex emotions, visualising your ideal relationship, or reflecting on past experiences, having extra space will give you the freedom to express yourself without limitations. Take your time, and let your reflections flow naturally.

Chapter 3

Reflecting on Emotional Wounds:
What past experiences or relationships have left emotional scars on your heart? How do these unresolved emotions manifest in your current thoughts, feelings, and actions? :

Chapter 4

Why Rebounding After a Dysfunctional Relationship is Unhealthy

Rebounding into a new relationship immediately after leaving a dysfunctional or abusive one can be deeply harmful to your emotional and mental well-being. According to neuroscience and psychological research, there are several key reasons why it's essential to avoid this and instead focus on healing before moving forward:

1. **Unresolved Trauma and Emotional Baggage:**
   - When you leave a dysfunctional or abusive relationship, you often carry unresolved trauma and emotional scars that need attention and healing. Jumping into a new relationship without addressing these issues can result in repeating unhealthy patterns. Your brain is still wired to react to the triggers and dynamics of the previous relationship, making it challenging to establish a healthy connection with a new partner.

2. **Impaired Decision-Making:**
   - After a toxic relationship, your brain is often in a state of heightened stress and anxiety. This can impair your prefrontal cortex, the part of the brain responsible for rational thinking and decision-making. As a result, you may make impulsive choices or settle for another unhealthy relationship, as your brain seeks comfort or validation rather than a truly compatible partner.

3. **The Cycle of Dysfunctional Relationships:**
   - Without proper healing, you are at risk of entering into a cycle of dysfunctional relationships. Your brain, having adapted to the chaos and dysfunction of the past, might subconsciously seek out similar dynamics in a new partner. This happens because your brain has not yet rewired itself to recognise and desire healthier relationship patterns.

The Importance of Deep Healing and Inner Child Work

Healing from a dysfunctional or abusive relationship requires deep inner work, including addressing past traumas and healing your inner child. Here's why this is crucial:

1. **Rewiring the Brain:**
   - Neuroscience shows that our brains are incredibly adaptable through a process called neuroplasticity. By engaging in deep healing practices, such as therapy, meditation, and journaling, you can begin to rewire your brain to release old patterns and form new, healthier ones. This process helps you become more resilient, self-aware, and capable of recognising and choosing a partner who aligns with your true needs and desires.

2. **Healing the Inner Child:**
   - The inner child represents the part of you that holds early emotional wounds, often from childhood experiences. These wounds can manifest as low self-esteem, fear of abandonment, or a tendency to seek validation in unhealthy ways. Healing your inner child allows you to break free from these patterns, fostering self-love and security from within, rather than seeking it from external sources.

3. **Building a Strong Foundation:**
   - Deep healing provides a strong emotional and psychological foundation. It helps you develop a clear sense of your worth and boundaries, enabling you to enter future relationships from a place of wholeness rather than neediness or fear.

How Long Should You Stay Single and Focus on Healing?

The duration of the healing process varies for each individual, but generally, it's recommended to stay single for a significant period after leaving a dysfunctional or abusive relationship. This time allows you to fully process your emotions, understand the lessons from your past experiences, and rebuild your sense of self. Here are some guidelines:

1. **Minimum Timeframe:**
   - It's often suggested to spend at least 6 months to a year focusing on personal growth and healing before entering a new relationship. This time frame allows your brain to begin rewiring itself and for you to establish healthier emotional patterns.

2. **Signs You're Ready for a New Relationship:**
   - You've processed the emotions related to your past relationship and no longer feel intense anger, sadness, or fear when thinking about it.
   - You've developed a strong sense of self-worth and no longer seek external validation to feel complete.
   - You're capable of setting and maintaining healthy boundaries.
   - You're excited about the idea of a new relationship, but not desperate for it. You feel content being single and understand that a partner would complement your life, not complete it.

Achieving a Truly Magical Relationship
Once you've done the necessary healing work, you'll be in a much better position to attract and cultivate a truly magical relationship. Here's how deep healing prepares you:

1. **Attracting Healthier Partners:**
   - When you heal and raise your self-awareness, you naturally start to attract partners who reflect your new, healthier state of mind. You'll be more likely to recognise and connect with people who share your values, goals, and emotional maturity.

2. **Building a Relationship on a Solid Foundation:**
   - With a healed heart and mind, you can build a relationship based on mutual respect, understanding, and love. You'll be better equipped to communicate effectively, resolve conflicts, and support each other's growth.

3. **Sustaining Long-Term Happiness:**
   - A relationship built after both partners have done their inner work is more likely to sustain long-term happiness and fulfilment. The emotional resilience and self-awareness gained through healing make it easier to navigate the challenges that naturally arise in any relationship.

In summary, rebounding after a dysfunctional relationship is unhealthy because it prevents you from addressing and healing the underlying issues that led to the dysfunction in the first place. By taking the time to heal, especially through inner child work and emotional processing, you set yourself up for a much healthier, more fulfilling partnership in the future. According to neuroscience, this deep healing rewires your brain to attract and sustain a truly magical relationship.

Journal Prompts

Here are some journal prompts designed to guide you through the healing process after leaving a dysfunctional or abusive relationship. These prompts will help you reflect on your past experiences, understand your emotional patterns, and prepare yourself for a healthier, more fulfilling relationship in the future.

1. Reflecting on Past Relationships
What recurring patterns or behaviours did you notice in your past relationships, especially the dysfunctional or abusive ones? How did these patterns affect your emotional well-being and sense of self?
This prompt encourages you to identify and reflect on the patterns that have repeated across your past relationships. Understanding these patterns helps you recognise how they have shaped your behaviour and emotional responses, allowing you to break the cycle in the future.

2. Understanding Your Triggers
What specific situations, words, or actions from your past relationships triggered intense emotional reactions in you? How did you typically respond, and how did these responses impact your relationships?
By identifying your emotional triggers, you can gain insight into the unresolved traumas that still affect you. This understanding is crucial for healing, as it allows you to develop strategies to manage and neutralise these triggers in future relationships.

3. Healing the Inner Child
Think back to your childhood. What early experiences might have contributed to the emotional wounds you carry today? How can you begin to nurture and heal your inner child?
This prompt helps you connect with your inner child, the part of you that may still hold pain from early experiences. By acknowledging and addressing these wounds, you can begin to heal and create a stronger, healthier sense of self.

4. Redefining Self-Worth
In what ways did your past relationships affect your self-worth? How can you redefine your sense of self-worth based on who you are today, rather than past experiences?
This prompt is about reclaiming your self-worth, which may have been diminished by past relationships. It encourages you to build a new, positive self-image that is independent of your past and rooted in your current strengths and values.

5. Visualising Your Ideal Relationship
What does a healthy, fulfilling relationship look like to you? What qualities do you want in a partner, and what qualities do you need to cultivate in yourself to attract this kind of relationship?
Visualising your ideal relationship helps you set clear intentions for the future. By defining the qualities you seek in a partner and the qualities you need to develop in yourself, you can align your actions and mindset with these goals.

6. Building Resilience
What steps can you take to build emotional resilience and ensure that you are not seeking a new relationship out of loneliness or fear, but from a place of wholeness and self-love?
This prompt focuses on strengthening your emotional resilience, which is essential for entering a new relationship from a healthy place. It encourages you to develop habits and practices that reinforce your self-love and emotional independence.

7. Setting Healthy Boundaries

Reflect on the boundaries that were either absent or crossed in your past relationships. What healthy boundaries do you need to establish in your future relationships to protect your well-being?

Setting and maintaining boundaries is crucial for a healthy relationship. This prompt helps you identify the boundaries that are important to you and how you can enforce them in future relationships to create a safe and respectful dynamic.

8. Exploring Forgiveness

What unresolved anger, resentment, or hurt are you still holding onto from your past relationships? How can you begin the process of forgiveness, for yourself and others, to release these burdens and move forward?

Forgiveness is a powerful tool for healing. This prompt encourages you to explore the process of forgiving yourself and others, which is essential for letting go of the past and creating space for a healthy, loving relationship in the future.

9. Creating a Self-Care Plan

What self-care practices can you implement to support your healing journey? How can these practices help you maintain emotional balance and prepare you for a healthy relationship?

This prompt guides you to develop a personalised self-care plan that supports your emotional and mental well-being. Regular self-care is vital for healing and prepares you to enter a future relationship from a place of strength and stability.

10. Defining Your Values

What are the core values that are most important to you in a relationship? How can you ensure that your future relationships align with these values?

Knowing your core values helps you attract a partner who shares and respects them. This prompt encourages you to clarify what matters most to you in a relationship and to use these values as a guide in your future choices.

These journaling prompts are designed to help you engage in deep reflection and healing after leaving a dysfunctional or abusive relationship. By working through these prompts, you can develop greater self-awareness, emotional resilience, and clarity about what you want and need in a future relationship, setting the stage for a truly magical and fulfilling partnership.

Journaling Instructions

In this chapter, you'll explore the importance of taking time to heal after leaving a dysfunctional or abusive relationship. Before jumping into new connections, it's crucial to process your experiences and emotions to ensure you don't carry unresolved trauma into your future. Use journaling prompts fro this chapter, and additionally use journaling as a powerful tool for healing:

1. **Daily Reflection:** Each morning and evening, take a few minutes to reflect on your thoughts, feelings, and progress. Write down any lingering emotions, fears, or thoughts that surface. This will help you process and release what no longer serves you.
2. **Identify Patterns:** Use your journal to identify any recurring patterns or thoughts that might indicate unresolved issues from your past relationship. Acknowledging these patterns is the first step toward breaking free from them.
3. **Set Intentions:** Write down your intentions for healing and personal growth. What do you hope to achieve emotionally and mentally over the next 12 months? How do you want to feel about yourself and your future relationships?
4. **Track Your Progress:** Regularly review your journal entries to see how far you've come. This will provide you with tangible evidence of your growth and healing, reinforcing your commitment to yourself.
5. **Express Gratitude:** Each day, write down something you're grateful for, focusing on the positive changes you're making. Gratitude helps rewire your brain to focus on the positive aspects of your life, which is essential for healing.

The Importance of Consistency: Daily Journaling for 12 Months

Consistency is key to achieving deep emotional and mental healing. Neuroscience and psychological research emphasise that lasting change and healing come from regular, sustained effort. By journaling daily for at least 12 months, you're creating new neural pathways in your brain that reinforce positive thinking and emotional resilience.

When you consistently reflect, process, and set intentions, you're essentially reprogramming your brain. Over time, this practice helps you release old, harmful patterns and replace them with healthier ones. The daily act of journaling keeps you connected to your healing journey, allowing you to track progress and stay focused on your goals.
Moreover, the habit of daily journaling strengthens your ability to self-reflect, which is crucial for maintaining healthy relationships in the future. By dedicating time each day to this practice, you're investing in your long-term well-being and ensuring that you approach future relationships from a place of strength and self-awareness, rather than from unresolved pain.
In summary, daily journaling is not just a tool for reflection, it's a powerful method for rewiring your brain, fostering self-love, and ultimately achieving the healing necessary to build healthy, fulfilling relationships in the future.

"Consistency in journaling rewires the brain, turning healing into a daily practice rather than a distant goal."

"True transformation happens through small, consistent efforts. Journaling daily for 12 months is a powerful way to reshape your mind and your life."

"Daily reflection through journaling helps you release old patterns and replace them with self-love and emotional strength."

Chapter 4

Reflecting on Past Relationships
What recurring patterns or behaviours did you notice in your past relationships, especially the dysfunctional or abusive ones? How did these patterns affect your emotional well-being and sense of self?

Chapter 5
Attracting Wrong People

Why We Keep Attracting the Wrong People and Stay in Dysfunctional Relationships?
The patterns of attracting the wrong people and staying in dysfunctional relationships, including potentially abusive ones, are deeply rooted in our subconscious mind, emotional conditioning, and self-perception. These patterns often stem from unresolved emotional traumas, low self-esteem, and ingrained beliefs about what we deserve in a relationship.

1. Unresolved Emotional Traumas
When we experience emotional trauma, especially in childhood, it can leave lasting scars on our psyche. These traumas can manifest in adulthood as patterns of behaviour where we unconsciously seek out relationships that mirror the dynamics of our past. For instance, if you grew up in an environment where love was conditional or where emotional neglect was common, you might find yourself attracted to partners who replicate these dynamics, perpetuating a cycle of emotional pain.

2. Low Self-Esteem and Lack of Self-Love
Low self-esteem and a lack of self-love are significant factors that contribute to staying in unhealthy relationships. When we don't value ourselves, we might believe that we don't deserve better or that we can't find a healthier relationship. This can lead us to tolerate disrespect, emotional abuse, or even physical violence, under the false assumption that this is the best we can get.

3. Familiarity and Fear of the Unknown
The brain is wired to seek familiarity, even if it is harmful. We might stay in a dysfunctional relationship simply because it feels familiar, and the brain perceives it as a safer option compared to the unknown of leaving and being alone. This is often why people find it hard to leave abusive relationships, there's a deep, subconscious belief that staying is less frightening than the uncertainty of leaving.

The Impact of Dating Apps on Mental Health

Dating apps like can amplify these issues by promoting a superficial approach to relationships. The instant gratification, constant swiping, and emphasis on physical appearance can lead to a range of mental health issues:

1. Superficial Connections
Dating apps often prioritise looks and first impressions over meaningful connections. This can lead to relationships that lack depth and emotional substance, making it easier for people to enter into relationships that are unhealthy or unfulfilling.

2. Comparison and Low Self-Esteem
Constant exposure to endless profiles can create a sense of competition and comparison, leading to feelings of inadequacy and low self-worth. If you're not getting as many matches or attention as others, it can exacerbate insecurities and reinforce negative self-beliefs.

3. Emotional Detachment
The nature of dating apps encourages a casual, disposable approach to relationships. This can lead to emotional detachment, where people become desensitised to rejection and the feelings of others, making it easier to engage in or tolerate unhealthy behaviours.

Becoming Amazing Before Attracting an Amazing Partner
Before you can attract a healthy, fulfilling relationship, it's essential to focus on becoming the best version of yourself. According to neuroscience and the insights in The Love Reset, here's how you can achieve this:

1. Healing Emotional Traumas
Start by addressing and healing any past traumas. This can be done through therapy, self-reflection, and journaling. Understanding your past is crucial to breaking free from unhealthy patterns and creating new, positive ones.

2. Building Self-Love and Self-Worth
Work on improving your self-esteem and self-worth. Engage in practices that affirm your value, such as positive self-talk, setting boundaries, and surrounding yourself with supportive people. Self-love is the foundation of any healthy relationship, and when you truly value yourself, you won't settle for less than you deserve.

3. Rewiring Your Brain
Use the principles of neuroplasticity to rewire your brain for healthier relationships. This involves creating new habits and thought patterns that support your goals. For instance, if you've always believed that you're not worthy of love, start challenging that belief and replace it with affirmations of your worth.

4. Cultivating Emotional Awareness
Develop emotional intelligence by becoming more aware of your emotions and how they influence your behaviour. This includes recognising triggers, understanding your emotional responses, and learning how to manage them effectively.

5. Setting Intentions for Relationships
Be clear about what you want in a partner and a relationship. Set intentions that align with your values and what you truly desire. This clarity will help you attract partners who are compatible with your goals and who respect and appreciate you.

6. Practicing Patience and Self-Care
Finally, be patient with yourself. Personal growth is a journey, and it takes time to change deep-seated patterns. Practice self-care and be kind to yourself as you work towards becoming the person who can attract and maintain a healthy, loving relationship.

Conclusion
In conclusion, attracting the wrong people and staying in dysfunctional relationships is often a reflection of unresolved issues within ourselves. To break this cycle, it's essential to heal, build self-love, and rewire our brains for healthier patterns. By doing so, we become better equipped to attract and sustain the kind of relationships that bring joy, fulfilment, and true love into our lives.

Journal Prompts for Healing and Attracting Healthy Relationships
To help you process and heal from past experiences, build self-love, and rewire your brain for healthier relationship patterns, here are some journal prompts based on the principles discussed in the previous chapter. Each prompt is designed to encourage deep self-reflection and facilitate emotional growth, helping you to attract and sustain a fulfilling and healthy relationship.

1. Reflecting on Past Relationships
Think about your past relationships. What patterns do you notice in the types of partners you've chosen and the dynamics of these relationships? What do these patterns reveal about your unmet needs, beliefs, or emotional wounds?
This prompt encourages you to examine your relationship history and identify recurring patterns that might be rooted in unresolved emotional issues. By recognising these patterns, you can begin to understand how they have influenced your choices and behaviours in relationships, setting the stage for change.

2. Understanding Your Emotional Triggers
What situations or behaviours in a relationship trigger strong emotional reactions in you? Reflect on the possible origins of these triggers and how they've impacted your relationships.
Emotional triggers are often linked to past experiences and unresolved traumas. By identifying your triggers and their origins, you can start to work on healing these wounds and prevent them from negatively affecting your current and future relationships.

3. Rewriting Your Self-Beliefs
List the negative beliefs you hold about yourself that might be affecting your relationships. For each belief, write a positive affirmation that counters it. How can you begin to internalise these new, empowering beliefs?
Low self-esteem and negative self-beliefs can lead to unhealthy relationship choices. This prompt helps you to challenge and replace those negative beliefs with positive affirmations, gradually shifting your mindset toward one of self-worth and self-love.

4. Visualising Your Ideal Relationship
Describe your ideal relationship in detail. What qualities do you and your partner bring to the relationship? How do you communicate, support each other, and grow together? What steps can you take to become the kind of person who attracts and sustains this relationship?
Visualisation is a powerful tool in rewiring the brain. By clearly defining what you want in a relationship, you can align your actions and choices with these desires, making it more likely that you will attract a partner who shares your vision.

5. Healing Emotional Wounds
Identify any unresolved emotional wounds that might be influencing your relationships. How can you begin to heal these wounds? What support or resources do you need to facilitate this healing?
Healing is essential for breaking unhealthy patterns. This prompt guides you to acknowledge and address emotional pain that might be holding you back, setting the foundation for healthier relationships in the future.

6. Practicing Self-Love and Self-Care
What does self-love mean to you? List five ways you can practice self-love and self-care daily. How will these practices improve your relationship with yourself and, consequently, with others?
Self-love and self-care are crucial for maintaining healthy relationships. By prioritising your well-being, you ensure that you have the emotional resources to contribute positively to a relationship without losing yourself in it.

7. Breaking Free from Familiar, Unhealthy Patterns
Have you ever stayed in a relationship because it felt familiar, even if it was unhealthy? Reflect on why familiarity felt safe and how you can embrace the unknown to create a healthier future.
The brain often seeks comfort in familiarity, even when it's harmful. This prompt helps you understand why you might be drawn to familiar but unhealthy patterns and encourages you to embrace change for the sake of your well-being.

8. Setting Boundaries and Standards
What boundaries and standards do you need to set in your relationships to protect your well-being and ensure mutual respect? How can you communicate these effectively?
Healthy boundaries are vital for any relationship. This prompt encourages you to define what you need in a relationship and how to assert these needs, ensuring that you attract and maintain relationships that are respectful and nurturing.

9. Cultivating Emotional Awareness
How aware are you of your emotions on a daily basis? Describe a recent situation where you reacted emotionally. How could you have handled it differently with greater emotional awareness?
Emotional awareness helps you to manage your reactions and communicate more effectively in relationships. This prompt encourages mindfulness in your emotional responses, leading to healthier interactions with your partner.

10. Commitment to Growth
What areas of personal growth do you want to focus on to improve your relationships? How can you commit to this growth, and what support will you seek along the way?
Growth is a continuous process in both personal development and relationships. This prompt encourages you to identify areas for improvement and to actively work on becoming the best version of yourself, which will, in turn, enhance the quality of your relationships.

Conclusion
These journal prompts are tools for deep introspection and personal growth, helping you to break free from unhealthy patterns and attract the loving, fulfilling relationships you deserve. By consistently reflecting on these questions, you can rewire your brain for healthier relationship dynamics, build self-love, and ultimately attract a partner who resonates with your higher self.

Use the journaling pages within this book to guide your reflections at the end of each chapter, and pair this with a separate notebook to journal twice daily. Morning journaling helps set your intentions, clarify your goals, and align your mindset for the day ahead. It activates the brain's prefrontal cortex, enhancing focus and decision-making. Evening journaling, on the other hand, allows for reflection on the day's experiences, processing emotions, and reinforcing positive neural pathways as you sleep.
By combining both practices, you're maximising the brain's ability to rewire itself toward emotional healing, self-awareness, and long-term well-being.

Chapter 5

Reflecting on Past Relationships
Think about your past relationships. What patterns do you notice in the types of partners you've chosen and the dynamics of these relationships? What do these patterns reveal about your unmet needs, beliefs, or emotional wounds?

Chapter 6
Dating with "Daddy Issues"

Dating with unresolved "daddy issues" can feel like navigating relationships with invisible baggage. These issues, often rooted in early childhood experiences, may stem from an absent, neglectful, or emotionally unavailable father figure. Neuroscience shows us that these early attachment wounds can shape the brain's wiring, leading to patterns of insecurity, fear of abandonment, or an unconscious attraction to unavailable partners in adulthood. In this chapter, we will explore what's happening in the brain, what's missing emotionally, and how you can heal these patterns to foster healthier, happier relationships.

When someone with "daddy issues" navigates the world of dating, their behaviour often stems from unresolved attachment wounds linked to their relationship with their father, or the absence of one.
Neuroscience sheds light on the deep-rooted patterns in the brain that drive this behaviour, what's missing, and, crucially, how to heal these patterns to create healthy and happy relationships.

What's Happening in the Brain:

1. **Attachment System Disruption:** During early childhood, our brain develops key attachment pathways based on our interactions with caregivers. If a father figure is emotionally distant, unavailable, or absent, it can disrupt the formation of secure attachment. The brain, specifically areas like the amygdala (which processes emotions) and the hippocampus (which forms memories), becomes wired to expect instability or rejection in relationships. This can lead to anxious or avoidant attachment styles in adulthood, where one either clings to or avoids intimacy out of fear of abandonment.
2. **Dopamine and Reward Systems:** The brain's dopamine system, which governs feelings of pleasure and reward, plays a key role in relationships. For those with "daddy issues," there is often a craving for validation and approval that wasn't received in childhood. The brain learns to associate emotional highs with the pursuit of unavailable or inconsistent partners, as it mirrors the unpredictability experienced growing up.

This creates cycles of unhealthy, dramatic relationships because the brain mistakenly interprets these emotional swings as passion.

3. **Prefrontal Cortex and Emotional Regulation:** The prefrontal cortex, which governs decision-making and self-regulation, can be underdeveloped when childhood attachment wounds aren't healed. This can result in impulsive behaviour, emotional outbursts, or difficulties in setting boundaries. Someone with "daddy issues" may subconsciously repeat toxic patterns in relationships, struggling to identify what a healthy dynamic looks like.

What's Missing:
- Emotional Safety and Stability: One of the core elements missing is a sense of emotional security. The person may have learned that love is conditional or inconsistent. Their brain craves the emotional safety they lacked, but without the tools to build it, they may fall into relationships that replicate the chaos or distance they experienced with their father.

- A Model of Healthy Love: Without a healthy example of love and trust from a primary caregiver, the brain lacks a template for what a stable, supportive, and nurturing relationship looks like. This can lead them to seek validation externally, believing their worth is dependent on someone else's approval.

- Self-Worth: Often, at the root of "daddy issues" is a diminished sense of self-worth. The brain has internalised the idea that they are not "enough" without someone else's love or validation. This leads to seeking partners who they believe can "complete" them, instead of approaching relationships from a place of self-assuredness and fulfilment.

What to Do About It:

- **Rewire Attachment Patterns:** Therapy, especially approaches like Attachment-Based Therapy or Cognitive Behavioural Therapy (CBT), can help individuals rewire their attachment systems. By understanding how their past affects their present relationships, they can begin to form healthier emotional patterns. Neuroscience has shown that neuroplasticity allows us to rewire our brains at any age, creating new, more secure pathways for attachment.

- **Practice Self-Love and Validation:** Begin by cultivating a strong, loving relationship with yourself. Techniques such as mindfulness and self-compassion exercises can help reframe internal narratives and boost self-worth. By learning to validate your own emotions, you reduce the need for external validation, and this rewiring changes how the brain processes self-worth and pleasure.

- **Recognise and Avoid Toxic Patterns:** Through self-awareness, identify the types of partners and relationships that trigger old attachment wounds. Journaling, therapy, and meditation can help bring these unconscious patterns to the surface. Neuroscience tells us that with awareness, we can actively choose different responses, creating new neural pathways that lead to healthier behaviour.

- **Establish Boundaries and Emotional Regulation:** Developing emotional boundaries is crucial. Working on the prefrontal cortex through mindfulness practices and emotional regulation techniques can help someone with "daddy issues" avoid impulsive decisions and regulate intense emotions. Setting boundaries creates a sense of emotional safety in relationships.

- **Seek Healthy Role Models:** Surround yourself with individuals and relationships that model healthy love and support. This can retrain the brain to expect stability and emotional safety, which over time rewires attachment systems. Neuroscience shows that observing healthy dynamics can reshape our own relational expectations.

- **Gradual Trust-Building:** For individuals with trust issues due to childhood wounds, learning to trust again takes time. It's essential to build relationships gradually, letting your brain and nervous system adjust to safe, stable affection. Oxytocin, the bonding hormone, is released through small, positive interactions over time, which helps build trust and security in relationships.

Conclusion:
To move from unhealthy dating patterns rooted in "daddy issues" to creating secure, fulfilling relationships, it's crucial to rewire the brain's attachment and emotional processing systems.

Self-awareness, self-love, and intentional action, the brain can form new, healthy pathways for connection, trust, and emotional stability. Healing the relationship with oneself is the foundation for transforming romantic relationships into sources of genuine happiness and growth.

Here are several journaling prompts along with explanations and suggested exercises to help process and heal attachment patterns related to "daddy issues," while cultivating self-love, trust, and emotional stability. These prompts are designed to facilitate deeper introspection and growth, based on neuroscience principles for creating healthier relationships.

Journaling Prompts:

- "What early memories do I have of my father (or father figure), and how do I think these experiences shaped my understanding of love and trust?"
  - Explanation: This prompt encourages reflection on how your early relationship with your father has influenced your current attachment patterns. By bringing these memories into conscious awareness, you can start understanding how they may be affecting your present relationships.
  - Exercise: Write for 10 minutes without stopping. Afterward, identify any recurring themes or emotions (e.g., fear of abandonment, need for validation). Reflect on how these themes show up in your romantic relationships today.

- "How do I feel when my partner (or a potential partner) shows me affection, love, or care? Do I feel worthy of this attention, or do I feel undeserving or anxious?"
  - Explanation: This prompt helps you examine your self-worth and emotional reactions to love and care. Often, people with attachment wounds struggle to feel deserving of love and may even feel anxious when receiving it.
  - Exercise: After writing, practice self-compassion by saying aloud, "I am deserving of love and care. My worth is not dependent on anyone else's approval." Repeat this exercise daily to help rewire feelings of self-worth.

- "What patterns do I notice in my past relationships? Do I tend to pursue unavailable or inconsistent partners, or do I feel anxious when someone gets too close?"
    - Explanation: This prompt guides you to recognise patterns in your dating history that may stem from unresolved attachment wounds. Awareness is the first step to breaking these cycles.
    - Exercise: Write out specific examples from past relationships where these patterns emerged. Then, ask yourself how you could have responded differently. Visualising a new response helps rewire the brain's habitual emotional reactions.

- "In what ways do I seek external validation in my relationships, and how can I begin to validate myself from within?"
    - Explanation: Neuroscience tells us that the brain craves dopamine when we receive external validation, but over time this can become a source of emotional dependence. Shifting to self-validation rewires the brain's reward system to be less dependent on others.
    - Exercise: Create a list of 5-10 things you love about yourself or moments you've been proud of. When you catch yourself seeking validation, revisit this list and remind yourself of your intrinsic worth.

- "What would it look like to create a relationship based on mutual support and trust, where both partners are secure in themselves? What would it feel like to experience this?"
    - Explanation: Visualisation prompts like this activate the brain's prefrontal cortex, which governs planning and emotional regulation. By envisioning a healthy, secure relationship, you create new neural pathways for what's possible.
    - Exercise: After visualising, write down actionable steps you can take to cultivate such a relationship. For example, "I will communicate my needs more clearly," or "I will work on regulating my emotions when I feel insecure."

- "How can I create stronger emotional boundaries in my relationships? What signs tell me that I'm giving too much or losing myself in a relationship?"
    - Explanation: Boundaries are essential for emotional regulation and maintaining individual identity in relationships. This prompt helps you reflect on where your boundaries may be too loose or non-existent, contributing to unhealthy dynamics.
    - Exercise: Write a "boundary script" for difficult situations (e.g., "When I feel overwhelmed, I will take time for myself without feeling guilty"). Practicing this script will reinforce healthier emotional responses in your brain.

- "How has my relationship with myself evolved over time, and what do I need to work on to feel more secure in my own identity?"
    - Explanation: Healthy relationships begin with a strong sense of self. This prompt encourages introspection on how your self-relationship has shifted and what areas need further nurturing.
    - Exercise: Write down three things you want to nurture in your relationship with yourself (e.g., self-care, confidence, emotional regulation). Set a weekly goal to work on each of these aspects and track your progress.

- "What would it feel like to fully trust someone in a relationship? What fears come up when I imagine this level of trust, and how can I work through them?"
    - Explanation: For those with attachment wounds, trusting others can feel daunting. This prompt helps you visualise what trust feels like while identifying the fears or barriers that prevent you from fully trusting others.
    - Exercise: Write down each fear that arises and then counter each one with evidence of how trust can be built gradually and healthily. For example, "I fear being hurt, but I can build trust slowly by observing consistent actions."

Journaling Instructions:
- **Set a Clear Intention:** Before starting each journaling session, set an intention. For example, "Today, I'm going to explore my past relationship patterns to better understand my attachment style."

- **Write Freely and Non-Judgmentally:** Let your thoughts flow without worrying about grammar, structure, or whether it "makes sense." This allows deeper insights to surface from your subconscious.

- **Time Your Sessions:** Set a timer for 10-15 minutes for each prompt. This keeps you focused and encourages you to dive deeply into the topic without distraction.

- **Reflect and Review:** After journaling, take a few moments to review what you've written. Highlight any key insights or recurring themes, as these are the areas that likely need the most attention and healing.

Suggested Exercises:
1. **Mindfulness and Meditation:** After writing, take 5-10 minutes to sit in silence. Focus on your breath, allowing any thoughts or feelings that surfaced during journaling to settle. This helps integrate the insights you gained into your nervous system and promotes emotional regulation.
2. **Self-Affirmations:** Based on your journaling, create 2-3 positive affirmations. For example, "I am worthy of love and trust," or "I honour my needs and boundaries in every relationship." Repeat these affirmations aloud each morning to help rewire your brain's neural pathways.
3. **Visualisation Practice:** Spend a few minutes each day visualising what a healthy, secure relationship feels like. Focus on how your brain and body react when imagining trust, mutual support, and emotional safety. This primes your brain to seek and create such relationships in real life.

By consistently engaging in these journaling practices, you'll begin to rewire your brain toward more secure attachment patterns and healthier, more fulfilling relationships. The power of neuroplasticity ensures that with conscious effort, you can reshape your emotional responses and cultivate the kind of love and connection you deserve.

Chapter 6

"What early memories do I have of my father (or father figure), and how do I think these experiences shaped my understanding of love and trust?"

"How do I feel when my partner (or a potential partner) shows me affection, love, or care? Do I feel worthy of this attention, or do I feel undeserving or anxious?"

....

....

....

....

....

....

....

....

....

....

....

Chapter 7
Dating Apps & Mental Health

The Impact of Dating Apps on Mental Health
Dating apps have revolutionised the way people meet and form relationships, but they can also have significant downsides. The constant swiping, emphasis on physical appearance, and instant gratification can contribute to a superficial approach to dating, leading to various mental health challenges.

1. Superficiality and Objectification
The focus on looks and quick judgments on apps like Tinder can reduce people to mere profiles, fostering an environment where deeper connection and understanding are secondary. This can lead to feelings of inadequacy, low self-esteem which was likely already vey low, and even depression, as users may start to see themselves and others as commodities rather than complex, valuable individuals.

2. Instant Gratification and Reduced Patience
The instant nature of dating apps where a match is just a swipe away can decrease patience in developing real-life relationships. This expectation of instant connection can make it difficult to invest time and effort in nurturing a meaningful relationship, ultimately leading to frustration and disappointment when real-life interactions don't progress as quickly.

3. Fear of Missing Out (FOMO)
With an endless supply of potential matches, users may develop a "grass is greener" mentality, always wondering if there's someone better just a swipe away. This can prevent people from fully committing to a relationship, causing anxiety and dissatisfaction.

4. Mental Health Impacts
The repetitive nature of swiping, especially when it leads to repeated rejection or unfulfilling interactions, can have a cumulative negative impact on mental health. Users may experience increased anxiety, depression, and a sense of isolation, despite the promise of connection that these apps offer.

Meeting people on dating apps is often associated with hookup culture, making it less likely to lead to long-term, healthy, and happy relationships. While there are exceptions, several factors contribute to the higher likelihood of these connections ending in breakups or divorces:

1. Focus on Physical Attraction:
- Surface-Level Connections: Dating apps like Tinder are primarily visual platforms, where people swipe based on photos. This encourages shallow, appearance-based judgments rather than deeper emotional or intellectual connections.
- Instant Gratification: The immediate nature of swiping fosters a culture of instant gratification, where users might prioritise short-term physical attraction over long-term compatibility.

2. Casual Dating Mindset:
- Hookup Culture: Many users on dating apps are looking for casual encounters rather than committed relationships. This can create an environment where long-term intentions are less common, leading to relationships that are more likely to be fleeting.
- Ambiguity of Intentions: It's often unclear whether someone is looking for a serious relationship or just a casual fling. This ambiguity can lead to mismatched expectations, causing frustration and disappointment.

3. Overabundance of Choices:
- Paradox of Choice: The vast number of potential matches can lead to a paradox of choice, where users are less satisfied with their selections and more likely to continue searching for someone "better." This mindset can undermine commitment and encourage a cycle of short-term relationships.
- Decreased Value of Each Match: With so many options available, each match can seem less significant, making it easier for people to move on quickly if challenges arise in the relationship.

4. Lack of Real-Life Interaction:
- Limited Initial Interaction: Conversations on dating apps are often brief and lack depth, making it harder to establish a strong emotional connection. This can lead to misunderstandings and unmet expectations when the relationship transitions to real life.
- Skipping Important Stages: The transition from online interaction to in-person meetings can skip important stages of relationship-building, such as getting to know each other gradually in a natural setting. This can result in relationships that are built on shaky foundations.

5. High Turnover Rate:
- Frequent Breakups: Relationships that begin on dating apps often have a higher turnover rate due to the casual nature of the platform. The ease of meeting new people can make it less likely for individuals to invest deeply in any one relationship.
- Increased Divorce Risk: For those relationships that do lead to marriage, the factors mentioned above such as the emphasis on physical attraction and the availability of alternatives can increase the likelihood of divorce.

6. Cultural Perception:
- Stigma of Online Dating: Despite becoming more mainstream, online dating still carries a stigma for some people, especially when it comes to serious relationships. This can create pressure on couples to conform to traditional relationship milestones, sometimes before they are ready.

While dating apps can lead to meaningful relationships for some, the platform's design and cultural norms often promote a hookup culture that prioritises short-term gratification over long-term commitment. The combination of surface-level connections, an abundance of choices, and a casual dating mindset can make it difficult to form and maintain a healthy, lasting relationship. For those seeking long-term happiness and stability in their relationships, relying solely on dating apps may not be the most effective strategy.

Where to Meet People Instead
To build deeper, more meaningful relationships, it is important to step away from the digital world and engage with people in real life. Here are some suggestions:
1. Social Events and Gatherings
   - Community Events: Attend local events like festivals, markets, or charity functions. These are great places to meet people who share your interests and values.
   - Workshops and Classes: Join classes or workshops that align with your hobbies, such as cooking, art, fitness, or writing. Shared activities naturally create opportunities for conversation and connection.
   - Volunteering: Get involved with causes you care about. Volunteering not only helps others but also connects you with like-minded individuals who share your passion for making a difference.

2. Social Circles and Networking
- Friends of Friends: Expand your social circle by attending gatherings where you can meet friends of friends. These connections often come with the added benefit of shared interests and values.
- Professional Networks: Attend industry-related networking events or conferences. Meeting someone in a professional setting can lead to relationships based on mutual respect and shared goals.

3. Physical Activities
- Sports and Fitness Groups: Join a local sports team, running club, or yoga class. These activities not only improve your health but also provide a natural way to meet people.
- Outdoor Adventures: Participate in group hikes, cycling trips, or nature walks. The shared experience of being in nature can foster deep connections.

How to Talk to People and Initiate Conversations in Real Life

1. Start with a Simple Greeting
- Be Approachable: A smile and open body language invite conversation. When you see someone you'd like to talk to, make eye contact and smile.
- Introduce Yourself: A simple "Hi, I'm [Your Name]" can be the perfect icebreaker. It's straightforward and opens the door to further conversation.

2. Find Common Ground
- Comment on Your Surroundings: Mention something about your shared environment, such as the event you are attending, the weather, or an activity you are both involved in. For example, "This is my first time at this event; have you been here before?"
- Ask Open-Ended Questions: Encourage the other person to share more by asking questions that require more than a yes or no answer. For example, "What do you think of this place?" or "How did you get into [activity]?"

3. Listen and Engage
- Active Listening: Pay attention to what the other person is saying and respond thoughtfully. Show genuine interest by asking follow-up questions.
- Share About Yourself: Don't just ask questions, share your thoughts and experiences as well. Balance the conversation to create a mutual exchange.

4. Be Genuine and Authentic
- Avoid Pretence: Be yourself rather than trying to impress. Authenticity is attractive and builds trust.
- Compliment Sincerely: A genuine compliment can be a great conversation starter. Focus on something you truly appreciate about the person, whether it's their smile, their enthusiasm, or their insight.

Steps to Take to Meet a Compatible Person in Real Life
1. Work on Self-Improvement: Before seeking a partner, focus on becoming the best version of yourself. Invest in personal growth, develop your interests, and build your confidence.
2. Know What You Want: Clarify your values, goals, and the qualities you desire in a partner. This will help you recognise compatibility when you meet someone who aligns with your vision.
3. Be Patient and Open-Minded: Building a meaningful relationship takes time. Be open to meeting different types of people and allow connections to develop naturally.
4. Practice Consistent Self-Care: Maintain a healthy lifestyle, including regular exercise, good nutrition, and mindfulness practices. A well-balanced life will make you more attractive and resilient in the dating process.
5. Develop Emotional Intelligence: Learn to manage your emotions, communicate effectively, and empathise with others. High emotional intelligence is key to forming and maintaining healthy relationships.
6. Set Healthy Boundaries: Be clear about your limits and respect the boundaries of others. Healthy relationships are built on mutual respect and understanding.

By meeting people in real-life settings and focusing on meaningful connections, you can avoid the pitfalls of superficial dating apps and cultivate relationships that are truly fulfilling and healthy for your mental well-being.

Journal Prompts

These journal prompts are designed to help you reflect deeply on the impact of dating apps like Tinder on your mental health and relationships, and to guide you in cultivating healthier, more fulfilling connections.

1. Reflecting on Superficiality and Self-Worth
How have dating apps influenced the way I perceive myself and others? Do I find myself focusing more on superficial qualities rather than deeper connections? How has this affected my self-worth?This prompt encourages you to explore the impact of dating apps on your self-esteem and how they may have shaped your perceptions of what is important in a relationship. Reflecting on these aspects can help you identify areas where you may need to shift your focus to build deeper, more meaningful connections.

2. Understanding Instant Gratification and Patience in Relationships
In what ways has the instant nature of dating apps affected my patience in relationships? Do I find myself expecting immediate results, and how does this impact my interactions with potential partners? This prompt helps you consider how the instant gratification offered by dating apps might be affecting your expectations and patience in relationships. By reflecting on this, you can begin to cultivate a more patient, long-term approach to building connections.

3. Addressing Fear of Missing Out (FOMO)
Do I often feel like there might be someone better out there? How does this fear of missing out affect my ability to commit to and invest in a relationship? What steps can I take to overcome this mindset? This prompt is aimed at helping you recognise the impact of FOMO on your relationship choices. By addressing this fear, you can work towards fully committing to and investing in relationships without constantly searching for something "better.

4. Exploring the Mental Health Impacts of Dating Apps
How do I feel after spending time on dating apps? Do I notice any changes in my mood, anxiety levels, or self-esteem? What can I do to protect my mental health while using these platforms? This prompt encourages you to assess the direct impact that dating apps have on your mental health. By becoming aware of these effects, you can take steps to limit or manage your usage of these platforms in a way that protects your well-being.

Chapter 7

Reflecting on Superficiality and Self-Worth

How have dating apps influenced the way I perceive myself and others? Do I find myself focusing more on superficial qualities rather than deeper connections? How has this affected my self-worth?

Chapter 8
The Path to True Love

In the journey to find true love, many men unknowingly chase attachment rather than love itself. When love is sought from a place of need, the relationships that form often reflect unhealed wounds from childhood. These unresolved emotional patterns can keep men trapped in cycles of dependency and emotional turmoil, preventing them from experiencing the depth of true connection.

This chapter delves into the neuroscience behind these attachment behaviours, exploring how early experiences shape the brain and how healing from within is the key to finding lasting, fulfilling love. By understanding the difference between attachment and love, and by cultivating self-sufficiency and emotional wholeness, a man can attract a partner who reflects his healed and empowered self, building a relationship based on mutual love, not unmet needs.

When we say a man will never find true love until he feels like he needs no one, we are talking about a profound shift in his internal state. True love can only be attracted when he steps into a space of wholeness and emotional self-sufficiency. Neuroscience shows us that our emotional needs and attachment patterns are rooted in the brain's early wiring. When we rely on others to fill emotional gaps, we are engaging in attachment, not love.

A man seeking love from a place of neediness is driven by unresolved childhood traumas, often tied to his early experiences with caregivers, particularly around attachment. The brain forms neural pathways based on these early interactions, and if he experienced insecurity, neglect, or emotional absence in childhood, those patterns can resurface in adult relationships. As a result, he attracts partners who push psychological buttons that reawaken those traumas, triggering anxiety, fear, or dependency.

When a man steps into emotional wholeness, he rewires his brain. The parts of the brain involved in fear (like the amygdala) are calmed, and areas like the prefrontal cortex, which govern self-regulation and higher reasoning, are strengthened. He no longer operates from a place of lack or need; instead, he exudes confidence, security, and unconditional love. This shift in energy changes the kind of partner he attracts. No longer drawn to partners who mirror his old wounds, he now attracts individuals who reflect his healed and balanced state. This is what neuroscientists refer to as the brain's plasticity, its ability to change and form new, healthier patterns.

The journey to true love is about letting go of neediness, healing inner wounds, and cultivating self-love so deeply that it radiates outward. When a man no longer needs love from someone else, but chooses to share his love from a place of abundance, he attracts relationships built on genuine connection, not attachment. His partner becomes a reflection of the love he has for himself, a mirror of his healed inner self. This is where true love begins.

When a man is seeking love from a place of need, his brain is operating in a state of attachment rather than true love. This attachment is often rooted in early childhood experiences, particularly unresolved emotional wounds from his formative years. The brain, especially in its early stages, is highly impressionable, and these experiences shape how it processes emotions, attachment, and relationships throughout life.

What's Going On in the Brain:
- Attachment Systems: When a man seeks love out of need, he is likely activating old attachment circuits in the brain, such as those connected to the amygdala (the brain's fear centre) and other emotional systems involved in seeking safety and validation. These attachment circuits were developed early in life, often in relation to his primary caregivers. If those early bonds were insecure, neglectful, or emotionally unstable, the brain will seek out relationships in adulthood that mirror those unresolved dynamics.

- Dopamine & Reward Pathways: When someone seeks validation and love from an external source, they activate the brain's reward pathways, particularly dopamine. This creates a temporary feeling of pleasure or satisfaction when receiving love or attention from another person. However, this is a fleeting feeling and often leads to cycles of dependency, because the brain craves more of this external validation to feel secure. It is a "quick fix" that doesn't address the underlying emotional wounds.

- Fear of Abandonment & Insecurity: Deep within the brain's limbic system, where emotions are processed, feelings of fear, abandonment, and rejection are stored. When a person seeks love from a place of need, they are operating from this emotionally reactive part of the brain, often unconsciously. This can lead to behaviours like clinginess, jealousy, and a fear of losing the relationship, as the brain's fear circuits are constantly triggered.

- Lack of Prefrontal Regulation: The prefrontal cortex, responsible for rational thinking, emotional regulation, and long-term planning, may not be fully engaged when someone is operating from a place of need. Emotional reactivity takes over, and the person struggles to maintain emotional balance. Without the ability to self-regulate, the relationship becomes driven by emotional ups and downs, rather than stability and mutual support.

What's Missing:
1. Self-Love & Emotional Security: The person is missing a foundation of self-love and emotional security. Neuroscience teaches us that emotional regulation starts within, when a person feels emotionally complete, their brain is balanced, calm, and self-sufficient. The absence of self-love means that they are relying on others to provide the feelings of security and validation that they should be cultivating internally.
2. Healthy Boundaries: When someone seeks love from a place of need, healthy boundaries are often lacking. The brain's attachment system is so focused on holding on to the relationship that it doesn't know how to create healthy space. This can lead to codependency and blurred emotional lines.

3. Internal Fulfilment: There's a gap in internal fulfilment, the brain is wired to seek external sources to fill emotional gaps. A truly healthy relationship requires both partners to feel emotionally fulfilled on their own, without relying on each other to meet all their emotional needs.

What to Do to Achieve a Healthy, Happy Relationship:
1. Build Emotional Independence: The first step is rewiring the brain to become emotionally independent. Practices like mindfulness, meditation, and self-reflection can help reduce emotional reactivity and strengthen the prefrontal cortex, which helps in regulating emotions. Over time, the brain learns to find joy and fulfilment within, rather than depending on external sources.
2. Cultivate Self-Love: Neuroscience shows that when you consciously practice self-love, you activate the brain's reward system in a healthier way. Engage in daily affirmations, self-care routines, and activities that foster self-compassion. This retrains the brain to release dopamine and oxytocin, creating feelings of contentment and security from within.
3. Rewire Limiting Beliefs: The brain holds onto limiting beliefs from early childhood, especially around love and worthiness. Cognitive-behavioural techniques (CBT) or working with a therapist can help you reframe these beliefs. For example, replacing "I need someone to love me" with "I am whole and complete on my own" can help rewire neural pathways over time.
4. Focus on Inner Healing: Childhood trauma and emotional wounds need to be healed. Therapy, journaling, and even neurofeedback can help the brain process and release stored emotional pain. Healing these wounds helps reduce emotional triggers, allowing the brain to form healthier, more balanced relationships.
5. Strengthen the Prefrontal Cortex: Emotional resilience comes from strengthening the prefrontal cortex. Practices like gratitude journaling, setting clear goals, and focusing on emotional regulation all enhance the brain's ability to maintain balance, especially in stressful or emotionally charged situations.
6. Shift from Need to Choice: Finally, to attract true love, you must shift your mindset from "I need love" to "I choose to share my love." When the brain operates from abundance rather than lack, it creates new neural pathways that attract healthier, more balanced relationships. In this state, the brain no longer craves validation but instead enjoys the mutual exchange of love from a place of wholeness.

By focusing on emotional independence, cultivating self-love, and rewiring the brain's old attachment patterns, a man can finally attract true love that reflects his healed and fulfilled self.

Journaling Prompts for "The Path to True Love"

Journaling Instructions
These prompts are designed to help you reflect deeply on your emotional patterns, relationships, and inner healing. Set aside 10-15 minutes for each journaling session, writing freely and without judgment. Allow yourself to explore any emotions or memories that arise as you answer each question.

1. What does "needing no one" truly mean to me?
   - Explanation: This prompt encourages introspection about what it feels like to be emotionally independent. By reflecting on this, you begin to understand the difference between emotional self-sufficiency and dependence on others for validation or love.
   - Exercise Suggestion: After journaling, take 5 minutes to practice mindfulness. Visualise yourself as whole and complete, feeling unconditional love radiating from within. Focus on the feeling of being enough as you are.

2. In what ways have my past relationships reflected unresolved emotional wounds from my childhood?
   - Explanation: This prompt guides you to connect past relationships with early life experiences, helping you recognise patterns of attachment, neediness, or emotional triggers.
   - Exercise Suggestion: Write a letter to your younger self, addressing any childhood wounds or unmet needs that you still carry today. This is not for anyone else to read, it's an act of self-compassion and healing.

3. How have I sought validation or fulfilment from my partners instead of from within?
   - Explanation: This prompt encourages you to explore the times you've relied on external validation in relationships. It helps you become aware of how often you seek outside approval rather than trusting your inner worth.
   - Exercise Suggestion: Create an affirmation to counter the need for external validation, such as "I am worthy of love and happiness, independent of others' opinions." Repeat this affirmation daily.

4. What would it look and feel like to be in a relationship where I am whole and complete on my own?
- Explanation: By visualising a relationship based on wholeness, you create a mental map for the type of partnership you desire. This prompts you to imagine the qualities of a healthy relationship built on mutual love, rather than emotional dependence.
- Exercise Suggestion: Write out a detailed description of this ideal relationship. Be specific about how you and your partner would interact, communicate, and support one another from a place of emotional security. Revisit this description regularly to stay focused on the qualities you want to attract.

5. What steps can I take to heal any unresolved emotional wounds and step into a space of unconditional love for myself?
- Explanation: This prompt helps you identify actionable steps to heal and cultivate self-love. It encourages a proactive approach to emotional growth and mental well-being.
- Exercise Suggestion: Create a personal growth plan. List concrete actions such as attending therapy, practicing mindfulness, engaging in hobbies you love, or setting boundaries in relationships. Make a weekly commitment to nurturing yourself emotionally.

6. How would my relationships change if I no longer sought emotional fulfilment from others?
- Explanation: This prompt helps you envision the shift that occurs when you stop relying on others for emotional fulfilment. It encourages you to reflect on how healthier dynamics could emerge when you're coming from a place of wholeness.
- Exercise Suggestion: Spend a day focusing on self-sufficiency in your interactions. Notice moments where you might typically seek reassurance or approval from others and instead provide it to yourself.

7. What aspects of my current relationship (or past relationships) have highlighted my emotional triggers? How can I use these experiences for growth?
   - Explanation: Triggers in relationships often stem from unresolved trauma or unmet needs. This prompt helps you identify those triggers and use them as opportunities for personal development.
   - Exercise Suggestion: After journaling, create a "Trigger Journal" where you write down your emotional reactions during conflicts or challenging moments. Use this to identify patterns and reflect on how you can respond differently in the future.

By regularly journaling on these prompts and engaging in the suggested exercises, you can begin to cultivate a sense of emotional independence, heal past wounds, and step into relationships from a place of wholeness and unconditional love.

Use the journaling pages within this book to guide your reflections at the end of each chapter, and pair this with a separate notebook to journal twice daily. Morning journaling helps set your intentions, clarify your goals, and align your mindset for the day ahead. It activates the brain's prefrontal cortex, enhancing focus and decision-making. Evening journaling, on the other hand, allows for reflection on the day's experiences, processing emotions, and reinforcing positive neural pathways as you sleep.
By combining both practices, you're maximising the brain's ability to rewire itself toward emotional healing, self-awareness, and long-term well-being.

"The journey to true love begins with healing the inner child. Only by addressing the emotional wounds of the past can a man break free from the cycle of attachment and discover love built on trust, not fear."

"Healing from within transforms how we experience relationships. Instead of seeking validation through attachment, a man grounded in self-love invites a relationship rooted in mutual growth and emotional security."

Chapter 8

What does "needing no one" truly mean to me?
After journaling, take 5 minutes to practice mindfulness. Visualise yourself as whole and complete, feeling unconditional love radiating from within. Focus on the feeling of being enough as you are.

Chapter 9
Attracting What We Are

The idea that we only attract a partner who is a reflection of ourselves is deeply rooted in both neuroscience and psychology. This concept suggests that the quality of our relationships mirrors our inner state our self-perception, emotional health, and unresolved traumas. Let's explore why this happens and why deep healing is essential before we can attract a truly amazing partner.

1. The Mirror Effect: Attracting What We Are
Neuroscience shows that our brains are wired to seek familiarity and comfort, often leading us to attract partners who resonate with our subconscious beliefs about ourselves. These beliefs are often shaped by our past experiences, emotional traumas, and our level of self-love. For example, if we harbour unresolved issues of low self-worth or fear of abandonment, we may unconsciously seek out partners who reinforce these feelings, perpetuating a cycle of unhealthy relationships.

- **Familiarity Bias:** Our brain's preference for the familiar can lead us to choose partners who mirror the emotional patterns we experienced in childhood or past relationships, even if they were negative. This is because the brain associates familiarity with safety, even when it's detrimental.
- **Projection:** We often project our unresolved issues onto our partners, expecting them to fill emotional voids or validate our self-worth. This projection creates relationships that are based on neediness or dependency rather than genuine connection and love.

2. The Role of Self-Love and Emotional Health

Self-love and emotional health are foundational to attracting and sustaining a healthy relationship. Neuroscience tells us that when we deeply value and care for ourselves, we activate the brain's reward system, leading to positive emotions and behaviours. This, in turn, radiates outward, attracting partners who are also emotionally healthy and capable of mutual love and respect.

- **Neural Pathways and Self-Perception:** Our thoughts and beliefs about ourselves create neural pathways in the brain. If we constantly think negatively about ourselves, these pathways become stronger, reinforcing feelings of unworthiness. On the other hand, positive self-affirmations and self-love practices can rewire the brain, creating new, healthier pathways that support a positive self-image.
- **Emotional Regulation:** Healing from past traumas and developing emotional regulation skills such as mindfulness and self-compassion help us manage our emotions more effectively. This emotional stability is crucial in relationships, as it allows us to communicate more clearly, set healthy boundaries, and engage in conflict resolution without resorting to destructive patterns.

3. The Necessity of Healing Emotional Traumas

Deep emotional healing is essential to breaking free from negative relationship patterns. Trauma, particularly when unaddressed, can lead to self-sabotaging behaviours, mistrust, and emotional reactivity, all of which undermine relationship success.

- **The Amygdala and Trauma Responses:** The amygdala, the brain's fear centre, becomes hyperactive when we have unresolved trauma. This can cause us to overreact to perceived threats in relationships, pushing partners away or creating unnecessary conflict.
- **Neuroplasticity and Healing:** Fortunately, the brain's ability to change known as neuroplasticity means that we can heal from trauma and reshape our emotional responses. Through therapeutic practices such as cognitive-behavioural therapy (CBT), mindfulness, and journaling prompts in this book, we can process past hurts, reduce the amygdala's reactivity, and foster a sense of inner peace and security.

4. Becoming the Partner You Wish to Attract

To attract an amazing partner, you must first become amazing yourself. This involves cultivating self-love, healing from past wounds, and developing emotional intelligence. As you grow and evolve, you naturally begin to attract partners who match your newfound sense of self-worth and emotional maturity.

- **Vibrational Alignment:** From a neuroscientific perspective, your brain's electromagnetic activity influences your thoughts, emotions, and behaviours. When you elevate your emotional state through self-love and healing, you emit a higher "vibration," which can attract others who are on the same emotional and energetic wavelength.
- **Self-Improvement as a Magnet:** As you work on becoming the best version of yourself through personal development, emotional healing, and cultivating inner peace you become a magnet for like-minded individuals who are also on a path of growth and self-discovery.

Conclusion: The Power of Inner Transformation

This chapter emphasises that the journey to attracting a loving, fulfilling relationship begins within. By addressing and healing your emotional traumas, cultivating self-love, and becoming the best version of yourself, you set the stage for attracting a partner who complements and enhances your life. The relationship you seek is not just about finding the right person but becoming the right person one who is capable of giving and receiving love at the highest level.

Why is Journaling so important?

Journaling is a powerful tool for self-reflection, emotional healing, and personal growth. By engaging with specific prompts, you can delve deeper into your thoughts, emotions, and behaviours, ultimately helping you understand yourself better and fostering the changes necessary to attract a healthy, fulfilling relationship.

Here are some journal prompts inspired by the themes discussed in the chapter on why we attract partners who mirror our inner state and the importance of self-love and healing:

Journal prompts:

1. Exploring Your Relationship Patterns
- What patterns do I notice in my past relationships? Do I tend to attract the same type of partner or encounter the same challenges? Why do I think this happens?
- This prompt encourages you to identify recurring themes in your relationships. By recognising patterns, you can begin to understand how your subconscious beliefs and unresolved issues might be influencing your partner choices and relationship dynamics.

2. Understanding Your Subconscious Beliefs
- What are my core beliefs about myself and relationships? Do I believe I am worthy of love, or do I have doubts? Where do these beliefs come from?
- This prompt helps you uncover the deep-seated beliefs that may be driving your relationship choices. Understanding these beliefs allows you to challenge and reframe them, which is crucial for attracting healthier relationships.

3. Reflecting on Past Emotional Wounds
- Are there past traumas or emotional wounds that I haven't fully healed from? How do these experiences affect my current relationships or my ability to trust and connect with others?
- This prompt guides you to confront unresolved traumas that might be impacting your ability to form and maintain healthy relationships. Writing about these experiences can be the first step in processing and healing from them.

4. Cultivating Self-Love
- What does self-love mean to me? In what ways do I currently practice self-love, and how can I improve? How do I think my relationships would change if I loved myself more fully?
- This prompt encourages you to explore the concept of self-love and assess how well you are nurturing yourself. It helps you identify areas where you can enhance your self-care practices, which is essential for attracting a partner who respects and values you.

5. Rewiring Your Brain for Positive Relationships
- What new habits or thought patterns can I develop to promote healthier relationships? How can I start rewiring my brain to attract the type of partner I truly desire?
- This prompt focuses on the concept of neuroplasticity the brain's ability to change and adapt. It encourages you to think about the positive behaviours and mindset shifts you can implement to create the relationships you want.

6. Setting Healthy Boundaries
- Do I set healthy boundaries in my relationships? Where do I struggle with boundaries, and how can I strengthen them to protect my emotional well-being?
- Boundaries are critical for maintaining a balanced and respectful relationship. This prompt helps you reflect on where your boundaries may be too loose or too rigid and how you can adjust them to improve your relationships.

7. Envisioning Your Ideal Relationship
- What does my ideal relationship look like? How does my partner treat me, and how do I treat them? What qualities do I need to develop in myself to attract and maintain this kind of relationship?
- Visualisation is a powerful tool that can help you align your desires with your actions. This prompt encourages you to clearly define what you want in a relationship and consider the personal growth required to achieve it.

8. Addressing Fear and Resistance
- What fears or resistances do I have when it comes to relationships? How do these fears hold me back from attracting the love I want, and how can I begin to overcome them?
- Fear is often a significant barrier to healthy relationships. This prompt allows you to confront your fears directly, which is the first step in reducing their power over your actions and choices.

9. Developing Emotional Awareness
- How well do I understand and manage my emotions in relationships? Are there specific emotions that often overwhelm me or cause problems in my interactions with others?
- Emotional intelligence is key to successful relationships. This prompt helps you evaluate your emotional awareness and regulation, offering insights into areas where you can improve to create more harmonious connections.

10. Committing to Growth
- What steps am I willing to take to heal, grow, and become the best version of myself? How can I hold myself accountable for this journey of self-improvement and relationship enhancement?
- Personal growth requires commitment and consistency. This prompt is about setting intentions and creating a plan for your ongoing development, ensuring that you stay on track in your journey toward attracting and maintaining a healthy, fulfilling relationship.

Conclusion

These journal prompts are designed to help you dig deep into your thoughts, emotions, and behaviours, ultimately leading to greater self-awareness and personal growth. By consistently engaging with these prompts, you can start to heal past wounds, challenge limiting beliefs, and cultivate the self-love necessary to attract and sustain a truly amazing relationship. The act of journaling itself also helps reinforce new, positive neural pathways, further supporting your journey toward lasting love and happiness.

Journaling Instructions

By regularly journaling on these prompts and engaging in the suggested exercises, you can begin to cultivate a sense of emotional independence, heal past wounds, and step into relationships from a place of wholeness and unconditional love.

Use the journaling pages within this book to guide your reflections at the end of each chapter, and pair this with a separate notebook to journal twice daily. Morning journaling helps set your intentions, clarify your goals, and align your mindset for the day ahead. It activates the brain's prefrontal cortex, enhancing focus and decision-making. Evening journaling, on the other hand, allows for reflection on the day's experiences, processing emotions, and reinforcing positive neural pathways as you sleep.

By combining both practices, you're maximising the brain's ability to rewire itself toward emotional healing, self-awareness, and long-term well-being.

Chapter 9

Exploring Your Relationship Patterns
What patterns do I notice in my past relationships? Do I tend to attract the same type of partner or encounter the same challenges? Why do I think this happens?

Chapter 10
Giving & Contributing

Entering a relationship with a "what's in it for me?" mentality can be a recipe for dysfunction and eventual breakup. This self-centred approach often leads to a relationship dynamic where both partners are more focused on taking than giving, resulting in a lack of mutual support, understanding, and growth. Here's why this mindset is problematic and how shifting to a mindset of giving and contributing can lead to healthier, more fulfilling relationships:

The Pitfalls of a "What's in It for Me?" Mentality
- Selfishness Breeds Discontent:
    - When one or both partners enter a relationship primarily focused on what they can get rather than what they can give, it creates a one-sided dynamic. This approach can lead to feelings of neglect, as the other partner may feel unappreciated or used.
    - Over time, this selfish attitude can foster resentment, mistrust, and emotional distance. The relationship becomes a transactional exchange rather than a loving partnership, which undermines the foundation of trust and mutual respect necessary for long-term success.

- Lack of Emotional Investment:
    - A relationship driven by self-interest often lacks the emotional depth required to sustain it through challenges. When both partners are more concerned with their own needs, they may neglect the emotional needs of their partner, leading to a disconnect.
    - Without emotional investment, conflicts are harder to resolve, and the relationship is more likely to falter when faced with difficulties.

- Imbalance and Inequality:
    - A "what's in it for me?" mentality creates an imbalance in the relationship. One partner may end up giving more, while the other takes without reciprocating. This imbalance can lead to frustration and a sense of inequality, which erodes the partnership over time.
    - Relationships thrive on reciprocity. When both partners contribute equally, they create a sense of balance and fairness, which is essential for long-term happiness.

The Importance of Giving and Contributing in Relationships

- Creating Mutual Fulfilment:
    - A relationship flourishes when both partners are committed to giving and contributing to each other's well-being. When you approach your relationship with a mindset of generosity and selflessness, you create an environment where both partners feel valued and supported.
    - This mutual contribution leads to a deeper connection and a sense of fulfilment that goes beyond superficial needs. It strengthens the bond and lays the groundwork for a lasting and meaningful relationship.

- The Role of Self-Improvement:
    - To truly give in a relationship, you must first invest in your own personal growth and self-improvement. Cultivating inner wisdom, self-love, confidence, and compassion allows you to bring your best self to the relationship.
    - When you are fulfilled and secure within yourself, you have more to offer. This self-awareness and growth enable you to contribute meaningfully to the relationship, enhancing both your life and your partner's.

- Unconditional Giving:
    - Unconditional giving, without expecting anything in return, fosters an environment of trust, love, and mutual respect. When both partners give freely, the relationship becomes a space where both individuals can thrive and grow together.
    - This approach builds a strong foundation for the relationship, making it resilient to challenges and capable of enduring over time.

A relationship built on the principles of giving, contributing, and self-improvement is far more likely to succeed than one based on taking or self-interest. By focusing on what you can give to your partner and the relationship, rather than what you can get, you create a dynamic of mutual support and love that leads to lasting happiness and fulfilment. Shifting your mindset from "what's in it for me?" to "how can I contribute?" is the key to building a healthy, balanced, and deeply rewarding relationship.

Journaling Prompts

- **Reflect on Your Current Relationship:**
  - How do you currently approach your relationship? Are you more focused on what you can get or what you can give?
  - What areas in your relationship could benefit from a shift in focus towards giving and contributing?

- **Identify Moments of Selflessness:**
  - Recall a recent time when you acted selflessly in your relationship. How did it make you feel? How did it impact your partner?
  - What are some small, everyday ways you can show love and support to your partner without expecting anything in return?

- Personal Growth and Contribution:
  - In what ways have you invested in your personal growth recently? How has this self-improvement allowed you to contribute more effectively to your relationship?
  - What areas of self-improvement could you focus on that would enhance your ability to give in your relationship?

- Understanding Your Partner's Needs:
  - What do you think your partner needs most from you right now? How can you meet those needs in a way that strengthens your bond?
  - How well do you understand what makes your partner feel loved and appreciated? What actions can you take to show them love in the way they best receive it?

- Commit to Unconditional Giving:
  - Write about a time when you gave something to your partner without expecting anything in return. How did this act of unconditional giving affect your relationship?
  - What can you do this week to practice unconditional giving in your relationship?

Journaling Instructions

- Set Aside Quiet Time:
  - Find a quiet moment in your day, preferably in the morning or before bed, to engage with these journaling prompts. This is your time for reflection and growth.

- Be Honest and Open:
  - Approach each prompt with honesty. The goal is to understand yourself and your relationship better, so allow yourself to be vulnerable and truthful.

- Daily Commitment:
  - Make journaling a daily habit. Consistency is key to deepening your self-awareness and transforming your relationship. Aim to write in your journal every day for at least the next 12 months.

- Review and Reflect:
  - Periodically review your journal entries. Reflect on how your mindset and actions have evolved over time and how these changes have impacted your relationship.

- Stay Focused on Growth:
  - Remember, this journaling practice is about growth, both personal and within your relationship. Stay committed, and over time, you'll notice positive shifts in your approach to giving, contributing, and building a lasting, meaningful connection.

Chapter 10

Reflect on Your Current Relationship:
How do you currently approach your relationship? Are you more focused on what you can get or what you can give? What areas in your relationship could benefit from a shift in focus towards giving and contributing?

Chapter 11
Happy Relationship

Can We Be Happy in Relationships?
Yes, we can truly thrive, be happy, and experience deep love and fulfilment in our relationships. If you have the desire to improve your relationship, you'll find ideas in this book that you can consider implementing.
The ideas, rituals, and habits presented in this chapter, and throughout this book have proven fruitful for millions of people who have implemented them, including myself. But before I dive into these strategies, let's discuss some common challenges people face in their relationships and how to overcome them.

The Trap of Complacency
Many couples, once settled into a serious, committed relationship or marriage, become complacent. They start to believe that now that they're together, they no longer need to put in effort. This mindset often leads to neglecting the care of their minds, bodies, physical appearance, mental and physical health, and spiritual growth. The spark that initially ignited the relationship dims as the effort to woo each other, plan regular date nights, and engage in spontaneous activities wanes. Over time, partners may begin to take each other for granted, becoming more like strangers or, at best, roommates.
It's not uncommon for people and families to live under the same roof but remain disconnected, more engaged with their smartphones and other digital devices than with each other. This disconnect can cause relationships to feel hollow, where each person barely knows the other.

The Importance of Continuous Growth
From a young age, we are taught the importance of hard work in school to achieve good grades, get into a good university, and eventually secure a good job. Even after we obtain a job or start a business, success demands continuous learning and improvement. We attend courses, seminars, workshops, read books, and seek out coaches or mentors all to enhance our skills, contribute more, and achieve better results. If we don't grow and improve regularly, we risk losing our job or business.

Interestingly, almost everyone I've worked with has expressed a deep desire for a meaningful relationship filled with happiness, profound love, and fulfilment.

So why do so many couples stop learning, growing, and improving once they enter a serious, committed relationship or marriage?

Logic tells us that if we want a happy and successful relationship full of love, joy, and fulfilment, or what I call "The Relationship Bliss" we must continue to learn, grow, and positively contribute.

The Effortless Effort at the Beginning

At the start of a relationship, we put our best foot forward and make a genuine effort, which, if you think about it, feels almost effortless. We do our best to woo our ideal partner. We greet each other with smiles, kisses, and long hugs. We make an effort to get up from the sofa and greet our partner at the door as soon as we hear the keys, even if we're in the middle of watching football or our favourite TV show. Our new partner is our priority, and everything we do comes from the heart.

We are effortlessly courteous, kind, loving, caring, compassionate, understanding, and supportive.

We feel as though we're falling in love; our hearts are wide open, and we experience deep happiness, even vulnerability. It may seem like the other person is responsible for these feelings, but

in reality, they are just a catalyst. The feelings of effortless, profound love that overflow from within us have always been there. However, to feel this kind of love consistently, we must first debunk a few myths and misconceptions.

Journaling Prompts to Enhance Your Relationship

Neuroscience teaches us that our brains are capable of rewiring and adapting through intentional practices. Journaling is a powerful tool that can help us harness this neuroplasticity to improve our relationships. Here are some prompts to guide you:

- **Reignite the Spark:**
    - Reflect on the early days of your relationship. What specific actions did you and your partner take to make each other feel loved and valued? How can you reintroduce some of these actions into your relationship today?
    - Revisiting positive memories can activate the brain's reward system, releasing dopamine, which strengthens your bond.

- **Overcoming Complacency:**
  - Identify one area where you feel you've become complacent in your relationship. What steps can you take to actively improve in this area?
  - Consistently setting and achieving small goals can boost motivation and create lasting behavioural changes by reinforcing neural pathways.

- **Fostering Connection:**
  - How often do you and your partner engage in meaningful, distraction-free conversations? Plan and commit to regular "tech-free" times to reconnect on a deeper level.
  - Quality time without distractions allows for the release of oxytocin, a hormone that promotes bonding and trust.

- **Continuous Growth:**
  - What new skills or knowledge could you acquire to contribute positively to your relationship? Consider areas like communication, emotional intelligence, or conflict resolution.
  - Learning and growth stimulate neurogenesis, the creation of new neuron's, which enhances cognitive flexibility and adaptability in relationships.

- **Effortless Effort:**
  - Reflect on what currently feels effortless in your relationship. How can you build on these strengths to foster even more positivity and connection?
  - Focusing on strengths and positive aspects of your relationship can reinforce positive neural circuits, making it easier to maintain these behaviours.

- **Debunking Myths:**
  - Write about any relationship myths or misconceptions you've believed in the past. How have they influenced your behaviour, and what new beliefs would you like to adopt?
  - Challenging and reshaping beliefs can lead to cognitive restructuring, allowing for more constructive and healthy relationship dynamics.

By incorporating these journaling prompts into your routine, you can tap into the power of neuroscience to foster a deeper, more fulfilling relationship. As you continue to learn, grow, and contribute positively to your relationship, you'll discover that true happiness and love are not just possible they are within your reach.

Journaling Instructions for Enhancing Your Relationship

In this chapter, you'll explore powerful ideas, rituals, and habits designed to help you thrive in your relationship. The journaling prompts provided will guide you through self-reflection and encourage continuous growth in your relationship. To maximise the benefits, it's essential to approach this journaling practice with consistency and commitment.

Why Consistency Matters: Consistency is crucial because the brain rewires itself through repeated practices, a process known as neuroplasticity. By journaling daily for at least 12 months, you give your brain the opportunity to form new, positive neural pathways. This ongoing process helps you overcome complacency, reignite the spark in your relationship, and foster deep emotional connections with your partner.

Daily Journaling Practice:
1. Set Aside Time: Dedicate a specific time each day, preferably in the morning or before bed, to complete the journaling prompts.
2. Be Honest: Reflect deeply and write truthfully about your thoughts and experiences. This is your personal journey toward improving your relationship.
3. Stay Consistent: Make journaling a daily habit. The more consistent you are, the more effective the practice will be in helping you achieve lasting positive changes.
4. Review and Reflect: Periodically revisit your journal entries to track your progress and identify areas for further growth.

By committing to this journaling practice, you're investing in the long-term health and happiness of your relationship. Through self-reflection and intentional effort, you can transform your relationship into a source of deep love, joy, and fulfilment.

Chapter 11

Reignite the Spark:
Reflect on the early days of your relationship. What specific actions did you and your partner take to make each other feel loved and valued? How can you reintroduce some of these actions into your relationship today? Revisiting positive memories can activate the brain's reward system, releasing dopamine, which strengthens your bond.

Chapter 12
Happy After The Honeymoon

We Can Be Happy in Relationships
Through consistent effort, mutual growth, and positive contributions, it is entirely possible to create a magical, joyful, and deeply fulfiling relationship that endures over time. However, to reach this level of relationship bliss, we must first challenge and debunk some common myths that hold many couples back from achieving lasting love.

Myth 1: The Honeymoon Period Only Lasts for the First Few Months of the Relationship

What if I told you that millions of couples around the world remain deeply in love with each other, not just during the first few months of their relationship, but for years or even decades? Many couples, even after 10, 20, 30, 40, or 50 years of marriage, continue to experience a profound sense of love, joy, and effortless connection. They live in relationships full of fulfilment, where love feels unconditional and deeply rooted, even after decades.

How do they do it?

While there is no one-size-fits-all answer, the ideas and principles discussed in this book have helped many couples, including me and my wife, experience sustained love and happiness over time. The key is recognising that true relationship bliss doesn't just happen on its own; it requires conscious effort, daily intention, and a shared commitment to growth.

Couples who maintain a deep and enduring connection know that love is an evolving journey. They understand that relationships require active participation from both partners. This means showing up every day with the intention to grow together, improve individually, and contribute positively to each other's lives. Love, when nurtured, doesn't have to fade but can deepen over time.

The Neuroscience of Sustaining Love

The brain is wired to respond to novelty and excitement, which is why the "honeymoon phase" feels so exhilarating. In the early stages of a relationship, the brain releases large amounts of dopamine, the "pleasure hormone", which creates the feelings of euphoria and excitement. This is why new love feels so intoxicating and effortless.

However, as the novelty wears off, dopamine levels may decrease, leading to the belief that the honeymoon phase is over. But here's the truth: with intention, couples can continue to spark joy and excitement in their relationship by deliberately creating moments of connection, surprise, and gratitude. By doing this, you can stimulate the release of dopamine again and keep that excitement alive.

Additionally, oxytocin, the "bonding hormone", plays a crucial role in creating emotional intimacy and trust in relationships. Oxytocin is released during moments of physical closeness, emotional vulnerability, and shared experiences. By fostering connection through affectionate touch, deep conversations, and spending quality time together, couples can keep the brain's bonding system engaged and continuously deepen their connection.

Creating New Neural Pathways for Long-Term Love

Over time, the brain forms new neural pathways that associate your partner with feelings of love, safety, and joy. This is crucial for sustaining a long-term relationship. As couples actively engage in shared experiences and nurture their emotional connection, the brain begins to hardwire these positive emotions. With consistent effort, your brain can associate your partner with love, joy, and fulfilment even years into the relationship.

One important aspect of maintaining a thriving relationship is the daily practice of gratitude and appreciation. Neuroscientific studies show that expressing gratitude activates the brain's reward centres and promotes feelings of happiness and satisfaction. Regularly acknowledging your partner's positive qualities and contributions strengthens emotional bonds and reinforces positive neural associations.

"You're one 'thank you' away from creating a love that lasts, here's why it works."

How I Did It: Creating New Neural Pathways for Long-Term Love with My Wife

In my journey with Nadia, my wife, I've discovered that long-term love isn't something that just happens, it's something we build, day by day, with intention. Neuroscience shows us that the brain forms new neural pathways through repeated experiences. Over time, these pathways hardwire feelings of love, safety, and joy toward our partner. This is exactly what Nadia and I have done, consciously and consistently creating those neural pathways that associate our relationship with happiness and fulfilment.

One thing I've learned is that shared experiences are essential to this process. When we engage in activities together, whether it's traveling, cooking, or simply enjoying quiet moments, our brains wire these experiences into memories filled with connection.
These shared moments activate areas in the brain linked to emotional bonding, reinforcing our love for each other.

But perhaps the most transformative tool has been the daily practice of gratitude and appreciation. Neuroscientific research shows that expressing gratitude literally rewires the brain's reward system, releasing dopamine and serotonin, the "feel-good" neurotransmitters.

Every day, I make it a point to acknowledge and express what I appreciate about Nadia, her kindness, strength, and humour. These daily acts of gratitude have created a positive feedback loop in my brain, deepening and reinforcing our love. But what's most important is that I'm expressing gratitude for her being, not just for things she does. When I say, "Thank you for being so amazing," it's an acknowledgment of who she is as a person, simply for existing in my life.

This type of unconditional appreciation strengthens our emotional bond. It tells her that my love and gratitude aren't based on her actions or what she does for me, but on the profound value she has just by being. This understanding between us has created a relationship of mutual love and respect, where both of us feel fully seen, valued, and reciprocate those feelings naturally.

When we express love and gratitude without conditions, the brain wires that feeling as something enduring and secure. It helps in forming neural pathways that associate the relationship with positivity, safety, and joy, making love an ongoing, resilient emotion. This is the essence of true emotional connection and long-term relationship success.

It's fascinating that even after years, the brain continues to adapt and create new neural connections when you consistently invest in your relationship. With each "thank you," each moment of shared joy, our relationship becomes stronger, and my brain associates Nadia with fulfilment and love more than ever before.

So, if you're in a relationship, consider this: what small, intentional actions can you take today to rewire your brain for lasting love? Start with gratitude, it has a profound effect on your brain, your relationship, and your overall happiness. It worked for me, and millions of couples and continues to enrich my relationship every day.

Effort Every Day Keeps the Spark Alive
The idea that love is a passive, fleeting feeling is a myth. Love, when practiced as a daily intention, can become a source of endless joy and fulfilment. Couples who have thriving long-term relationships recognise that love is an action. They wake up every day with the intention to cherish and nurture each other.

It's important to recognise that happiness in a relationship doesn't come from grand gestures or occasional moments of connection but from small, consistent efforts to stay emotionally attuned to each other. Whether it's sending a loving text, sharing a meaningful conversation, or simply holding hands, these daily acts of love reinforce the emotional bonds that keep a relationship strong.

Conclusion: Sustaining Love for a Lifetime
To achieve lasting love and happiness, it's essential to debunk the myth that love fades after the honeymoon phase. By making daily efforts, creating meaningful connections, and understanding the neuroscience behind emotional bonding, couples can experience a love that deepens and flourishes over time.

Through these principles, you can cultivate a relationship filled with joy, fulfilment, and lasting intimacy, no matter how many years you've been together. With effort and intention, the honeymoon phase can last a lifetime.

Journaling Prompts for Sustained Love Beyond the Honeymoon Period:

- What are my current beliefs about the honeymoon period in relationships? Do I believe that the initial spark of love inevitably fades over time, or do I think it's possible to sustain passion and joy in a relationship for the long term?
    - Reflection Tool: Identify any limiting beliefs that may hold you back from embracing long-lasting love and fulfilment in your relationships.

- In what ways can I show intentional love and effort toward my partner, even after the "honeymoon phase" is over? How can I make this a daily practice?
    - Action Tool: Develop a list of small daily actions you can take to keep the connection alive and sustain a sense of joy and fulfilment in your relationship.

- How do I define unconditional love? In what ways do I currently practice unconditional love with my partner, and how can I expand on this practice?
    - Reflection Tool: Use this journaling prompt to deepen your understanding of unconditional love and its application in your relationship.

- What are the areas of my relationship that feel effortless and joyful right now? What practices or habits can I put in place to continue fostering this effortlessness over time?
    - Growth Tool: Create a plan to nurture the aspects of your relationship that feel natural and joyful, ensuring these elements remain central to your connection.

- What are the challenges or areas of growth in my relationship? How can I and my partner work together to address these challenges in a way that strengthens our bond?
    - Action Tool: Write about proactive steps you can take with your partner to turn challenges into opportunities for deeper growth and connection.

- How do I prioritise personal growth alongside relationship growth? In what ways can my individual growth positively impact my partnership?
    - Growth Tool: Write down areas of personal development that can help you bring your best self into the relationship, leading to sustained love and happiness.

- What rituals, traditions, or experiences can my partner and I create that celebrate our connection and help us stay in love over time?
    - Action Tool: Brainstorm meaningful rituals or practices you and your partner can implement to create lasting memories and reinforce the bond between you.

- How does neuroscience explain the shift in feelings from the early stages of love to long-term partnership? How can I use this understanding to foster a lasting, joyful relationship?
    - Learning Tool: Write down your understanding of how love evolves on a neurological level, and reflect on how this knowledge can help you build a more enduring connection.

- What have I learned from observing couples who have sustained love for decades? What qualities or habits do they exhibit that I can integrate into my own relationship?
    - Inspiration Tool: Reflect on role models for lasting love in your life and note the key lessons you can apply to your own partnership.

- How can I practice gratitude for my partner and the relationship on a regular basis? How does expressing appreciation influence the longevity of love?
    - Action Tool: Create a gratitude journaling practice specifically for your relationship, noting the ways your partner enhances your life and how expressing this gratitude strengthens your bond.

Additional Tools for Achieving Sustained Love:

- Daily Intentions: Set a daily intention to contribute positively to your relationship, focusing on actions like communication, support, and affection.
- Gratitude Practices: Incorporate gratitude for your partner into your daily routine, focusing on what you appreciate in them and how this fosters long-term joy.
- Rituals for Connection: Design weekly or monthly rituals that keep the romance alive, such as dedicated date nights, check-ins, or shared hobbies that bring you closer.

By using these journaling prompts, you will uncover insights about your beliefs, patterns, and opportunities for growth, allowing you to foster a long-lasting, joyful, and fulfilling relationship well beyond the initial "honeymoon phase."

Journaling Instructions for Reflecting on Relationship Longevity and Sustained Love

Journaling is a powerful tool to deepen your understanding of relationships and explore ways to nurture long-lasting love. The prompts below are designed to help you reflect on myths about the "honeymoon period" and how to foster ongoing connection, joy, and growth in your relationship. As you journal, keep the following instructions in mind to get the most from this process:

Journaling Instructions:
- Create a Quiet Space:
    - Find a calm environment where you won't be interrupted for 10–20 minutes.
    - Set an intention to be honest and open as you explore the questions. Allow yourself to be vulnerable in your writing.

- Write Without Judgment:
    - Let your thoughts flow freely. Don't worry about grammar, structure, or how your thoughts sound, just write.
    - Be compassionate and kind to yourself as you explore your beliefs, feelings, and experiences.

- Use Mindfulness as You Write:
    - Stay present in the moment as you write. If any strong emotions come up, pause and take a deep breath before continuing.
    - Reflect deeply on each question before you begin writing your response. Engage with your feelings as much as your thoughts.
- Take Your Time:
    - There's no need to rush. If you feel the need to pause or revisit the prompts later, that's fine. Give yourself the space to process deeply.
- Review and Reflect:
    - Once you've finished, read through what you've written. Notice any patterns or recurring themes. These can be areas where you might need growth or deeper exploration.

Journaling Prompts:
- Reflect on the Honeymoon Phase Myth:
    - How do you perceive the idea that the "honeymoon phase" of a relationship must fade over time? Do you believe that lasting love is possible beyond the first few months?
    - How has your experience in past or current relationships challenged or supported this myth?

- Sustained Love in Relationships:
    - What does "sustained love" mean to you? Describe how you envision love that lasts 10, 20, or even 50 years.
    - What qualities do you think are necessary to maintain profound love over the long term?

- Neuroscience and Relationship Growth:
    - From a neuroscience perspective, we know that the brain's reward system thrives on novelty and connection. How can you and your partner create new experiences together to nurture the "reward system" in your relationship?
    - What are some small daily practices you can implement to grow and maintain your emotional connection?

- Commitment to Daily Effort:
  - Reflect on the idea that relationship bliss requires daily effort. How do you and your partner currently contribute to each other's happiness and growth?
  - In what ways could you improve in supporting each other's personal and shared goals?

- Exploring Unconditional Love:
  - What does unconditional love look like in your relationship? Reflect on how you practice or experience love without conditions or expectations.
  - How can you foster more unconditional love for yourself and your partner? Are there any barriers or fears that prevent you from doing so?

- Emotional Fulfilment:
  - When you think of long-lasting love, what role does emotional fulfilment play? How fulfilled do you feel emotionally in your current relationship, and how do you contribute to your partner's emotional well-being?
  - Reflect on areas where you feel emotionally lacking, and brainstorm ways to increase fulfilment.

By using these prompts to explore your beliefs, feelings, and experiences with love, you'll gain deeper insights into what it takes to sustain lasting, joyful relationships.

"True love matures when gratitude extends beyond the honeymoon phase. It's about finding joy in the small, everyday gestures, and continuing to see your partner as a gift even after the initial excitement fades."

"After the honeymoon period, it's easy to take each other for granted. But when we intentionally practice gratitude every day, we reignite the spark and cultivate a love that goes far beyond the surface."

Chapter 12

Honeymoon period:
What are my current beliefs about the honeymoon period in relationships? Do I believe that the initial spark of love inevitably fades over time, or do I think it's possible to sustain passion and joy in a relationship for the long term?

Chapter 13
Busy after the honeymoon

Myth 2: After the Honeymoon Period, "I'm Just Too Busy" to Keep the Relationship Strong

Many people fall into the trap of believing that once the honeymoon period is over, they're too busy or too tired to maintain the same level of energy and effort in their relationship. They say, "I just don't have the time or energy to do what's needed for a fantastic relationship."
In my coaching work, I've met many clients including relationship coaches and therapists who believed in this myth. But when we take a closer look, we often find that people aren't really too busy; they're just prioritising the wrong things.

Consider this: You may feel like you don't have time, but if you tally the hours you spend scrolling through social media or watching your favourite shows, you'll often find 20-30 hours a week dedicated to these activities. That's more than enough time to focus on nurturing your relationship instead.

Neuroscience Insight:

The brain is capable of rewiring itself, even in the context of habits and priorities. By consciously choosing to shift your focus from distractions to your partner, you can strengthen the neural pathways that associate effort with emotional reward. Building habits of connection, even in small ways, trains the brain to prioritise your relationship.

Journaling Prompt:

- **Identify Time Leaks:** Track your daily activities for one week. How much time are you spending on social media, watching TV, or engaging in other low-priority activities? Write about what you've discovered.
    - Neuroscience Connection: Awareness is the first step to rewiring the brain. Identifying unproductive habits creates an opportunity to replace them with relationship-nurturing activities.

- **Reclaim Your Relationship Time**: List three activities you can reduce or eliminate to make time for connecting with your partner. How will you use this extra time to invest in your relationship?
  - Neuroscience Connection: Replacing old habits with intentional relationship-building practices strengthens positive neural connections, increasing your sense of fulfilment.

Journaling Instructions

On the following pages, take the time to answer the questions from the journaling prompts provided in this chapter. These prompts are designed to help you reflect deeply on your relationship, uncover new insights, and foster greater understanding between you and your partner.

Use the journaling pages within this book to guide your reflections at the end of each chapter, and pair this with a separate notebook to journal twice daily. Morning journaling helps set your intentions, clarify your goals, and align your mindset for the day ahead. It activates the brain's prefrontal cortex, enhancing focus and decision-making. Evening journaling, on the other hand, allows for reflection on the day's experiences, processing emotions, and reinforcing positive neural pathways as you sleep.

By combining both practices, you're maximising the brain's ability to rewire itself toward emotional healing, self-awareness, and long-term well-being.

"Your relationship deserves more than what's left after the busyness of life. Make it a priority, and watch it grow stronger every day."

Chapter 13

Identify Time Leaks:
Track your daily activities for one week. How much time are you spending on social media, watching TV, or engaging in other low-priority activities? Write about what you've discovered.

Chapter 14
My Other Half

The Problem with "Half Looking for Another Half"

Instead of thinking, "I'm a half looking for my other half," focus on completing yourself. Otherwise, what you're really chasing is attachment and craving. Many toxic relationships persist even when both people know they're unhealthy because, despite the toxicity, it feels better than being a "sad little half."

To truly experience love, it takes two whole people coming together, creating a synergy. So ask yourself this crucial question: If I were to be alone forever, could I be okay with that? If that question triggers discomfort or anxiety, that's something to process and release. The goal is to reach a place where being alone doesn't bother you, where you're at peace with it.

Being okay with being alone doesn't mean your goal is to stay alone. You can have the intention to be in a relationship while also being content with yourself. That's a healthy foundation. It's saying, "I'm complete, I'm okay with myself. My intention is to find a relationship, and if it happens, great. If not, that's okay too." This mindset eliminates neediness.

If you feel your partner "enhances" or "completes" you, that's the start of a toxic relationship. Think of the Disney movie model where two halves come together through "the power of love." It's toxic because it sends the message that without that partner, without that soulmate or twin flame, you're incomplete. Even if you do get the relationship, what follows? Neediness, craving, and fear of loss.

For example, if I believe someone like John completes me, I'd obsess over him. I'd be saying, "I need John. Without John, I'm nothing." I'd be crying over it, dreaming about him, consumed by the thought that without John, I'm incomplete. If John and I got together, I'd be constantly asking, "Do you love me, John?" He'd say, "Yes, I do," and I'd feel enhanced and complete for a moment. But what would happen the second after that? I'd fear losing him, because without John, I'd go back to being incomplete. That's how neediness morphs into fear of loss, creating a cycle of dependency and insecurity.

From a neuroscience perspective, this craving and fear activates parts of the brain involved in attachment, reward, and anxiety, reinforcing toxic emotional patterns. True wholeness comes when you're complete on your own, and relationships become an enhancement to an already fulfilled life.

The idea of being "a half looking for another half" stems from a deeply ingrained belief that we are incomplete on our own and need someone else to make us whole. This concept creates unhealthy relationships rooted in attachment, craving, and dependency rather than genuine connection. From a neuroscience perspective, this idea of neediness, attachment, and craving can be understood through the brain's reward and emotional regulation systems.

The Problem with "Half Looking for Another Half"
When we view ourselves as incomplete, our brain is essentially wired for constant **craving**. In this mindset, we are chasing external validation and attachment to fulfil an internal void. The brain's reward centre, specifically the ventral tegmental area (VTA), is a midbrain structure that plays a key role in reward, motivation, and addiction, becomes activated when we seek out something that gives us pleasure, such as love or attention. This can create an addictive cycle similar to substance dependency because the dopamine system is engaged in the anticipation of feeling whole or complete through another person.

In toxic relationships, the brain's **fear centres**, like the **amygdala**, become more active due to the constant fear of losing the person who is perceived as completing you. This keeps the body in a state of **stress and anxiety** because there's a deep-rooted belief that without the partner, you'll revert to being incomplete. The fear of loss triggers a stress response involving **cortisol**, the body's primary stress hormone. Over time, this can create a toxic loop of **neediness, fear, and anxiety.**

Toxic Relationships: Why They Persist
Toxic relationships often persist despite being unhealthy because, neurologically, the brain becomes **attached** to the intermittent reward. Even if the relationship brings pain, the idea of being alone and "incomplete" feels worse than the toxicity itself. The brain's reward system keeps reinforcing the attachment because being with someone, even in a harmful dynamic, still triggers those fleeting moments of dopamine and temporary relief from fear and loneliness.

In these situations, the **attachment system** is activated through the release of oxytocin during interactions with a partner. Oxytocin is often called the "love hormone" because it promotes bonding. However, in toxic relationships, this bonding hormone creates an unhealthy attachment, making it hard to leave even when the relationship is harmful.

The Importance of Wholeness: Two Whole People Coming Together
The healthier model for relationships involves two people who see themselves as complete individuals. Neuroscience shows that **self-regulation**, or the ability to regulate your emotions and thoughts independently, is critical for maintaining balanced and healthy connections. The **prefrontal cortex**, responsible for rational decision-making and emotional control, plays a significant role here. People who have developed self-love and emotional regulation are more likely to create healthy, secure relationships because they are not driven by constant craving or attachment.

By being okay with the idea of being alone, the brain achieves a state of **equilibrium.** This means that you are no longer dependent on external validation or the dopamine rush of new love. Instead, you can engage in relationships from a place of **wholeness and balance**, where love becomes an **extension** of your well-being rather than the foundation of it.

How to Achieve Wholeness: Facing the Fear of Being Alone
To move from a state of neediness to wholeness, you must confront and process any discomfort or fear around being alone. If the idea of being alone triggers anxiety or fear, that's a sign of unmet emotional needs that have been suppressed. This fear is largely driven by the brain's fear circuitry, particularly the amygdala, which associates loneliness with danger or inadequacy. By confronting these fears and working through them, you can rewire your brain's response to solitude, turning it into a peaceful and fulfilling state.

Through practices such as mindfulness and self-awareness, the prefrontal cortex becomes stronger, allowing for better emotional regulation and less dependence on external sources of validation. Over time, this reconditioning creates a new default state where love is not about fulfilling a void but about enhancing an already fulfilling life.

Eliminating Neediness: The Shift to Secure Love

When you are whole, love no longer becomes a source of need or craving, but rather an amplification of an already secure and fulfilled life. The fear of loss diminishes because your self-worth is no longer tied to the presence of another person. This creates a sense of security in relationships, where love is experienced as shared joy rather than a desperate need.

In a secure relationship, both partners are independently complete and can experience what neuroscientists call secure attachment. This form of attachment is supported by balanced levels of oxytocin and the ability to engage the prefrontal cortex for rational thinking, even when emotions are high. Secure attachment leads to relationships where there is mutual support, respect, and growth, without the underlying fear of loss or inadequacy.

The Toxicity of "You Complete Me"

The popular idea that someone else "completes" you, often romanticised in movies, leads to the activation of the brain's fear and reward systems in a detrimental way. When you believe someone else makes you whole, you place them in control of your happiness, and your brain becomes wired to avoid losing them at all costs. The constant fear of loss leads to obsessive thinking (driven by the caudate nucleus) and anxiety, keeping you in a state of emotional dependence.

Conclusion: A Neuroscientific Approach to Love and Wholeness
The healthiest relationships emerge when both individuals are emotionally complete and independent. Instead of craving another person to fill an emotional void, love becomes a synergistic experience where both partners enhance each other's lives without fear or dependency. By working through fears of being alone and cultivating self-love, you can rewire your brain to experience love as a fulfilling and balanced force rather than a need-driven craving. This approach promotes emotional health, resilience, and the potential for truly secure and lasting relationships.

Journaling Prompts

for Achieving Wholeness and Eliminating Neediness in Relationships
- What emotions or fears arise when you imagine being alone for an extended period?
  - Journaling Instructions: Explore your immediate thoughts and feelings about solitude. Write about the emotions this scenario brings up (e.g., fear, anxiety, or peace). Dig deeper into why these emotions surface and reflect on what this reveals about your sense of self and attachment.

- In what ways do you seek external validation to feel complete?
  - Journaling Instructions: Identify situations where you rely on others, whether through relationships, achievements, or approval, to validate your sense of self-worth. Write down specific examples and examine how this dependency impacts your emotional well-being and sense of wholeness.

- Reflect on past or current relationships: Were/Are you seeking completion from your partner?
  - Journaling Instructions: Think about your role in past or current relationships. Did you expect your partner to "complete" you? How did this affect the dynamics of the relationship? Write about how your mindset either contributed to or detracted from the health of the relationship.

- What does being "whole" mean to you, and how can you cultivate this within yourself?
  - Journaling Instructions: Define what it means to be whole and independent. List the qualities or habits you think you need to develop to reach a state of emotional completeness. Explore practices like mindfulness, self-care, or boundary-setting, and how these can help cultivate self-love.

- How would your relationships change if you approached them from a place of wholeness?
  - Journaling Instructions: Visualise a relationship where both you and your partner are emotionally complete and independent. Describe how this relationship would differ from one based on neediness or dependency. Reflect on how you can shift towards this healthier dynamic in future or current relationships.

Journaling Instructions
When journaling, find a quiet, comfortable space where you won't be interrupted. Begin by setting an intention for your journaling session, focusing on self-awareness and reflection. Use these prompts to guide your writing, but allow yourself to explore whatever thoughts and feelings come up. Be honest with yourself, journaling is a personal process, and there's no need to censor your thoughts. Spend at least 10-15 minutes on each prompt, and if emotions arise, sit with them, process them, and explore how they inform your sense of self.

Consider revisiting your entries over time. As you develop more self-awareness, you may discover new insights or shift perspectives.

This practice will help you rewire your brain to embrace wholeness and release the neediness that can lead to unhealthy attachment in relationships.

Use the journaling pages within this book to guide your reflections at the end of each chapter, and pair this with a separate notebook to journal twice daily. Morning journaling helps set your intentions, clarify your goals, and align your mindset for the day ahead. It activates the brain's prefrontal cortex, enhancing focus and decision-making. Evening journaling, on the other hand, allows for reflection on the day's experiences, processing emotions, and reinforcing positive neural pathways as you sleep.

By combining both practices, you're maximising the brain's ability to rewire itself toward emotional healing, self-awareness, and long-term well-being.

"Looking for someone to complete you is a recipe for disappointment. Instead, focus on becoming whole within yourself and love will enhance, not complete, your life."

Chapter 14

What does it mean to be "whole" in a relationship?

Reflect on your personal understanding of wholeness. How would your relationships change if you truly believed you were already complete?

....

....

....

....

....

....

....

....

....

....

....

....

....

Chapter 15
They Have To Make Me Happy

Myth 4: "It's My Partner's Responsibility to Make Me Happy"
This myth often goes hand-in-hand with the idea that our partner is our "other half." Many people believe that it's their partner's job to make them happy, to fill their emotional needs, and to fix their problems. However, this belief is not only unrealistic, but it also puts undue pressure on the relationship.

The Reality: Happiness Is an Inside Job
No one else can make you feel anything, your feelings are your own. Neuroscience shows that our emotions are the result of complex neural processes that occur within us, not something someone else can control. While your partner can support you and share life's journey with you, they are not responsible for your happiness. That responsibility lies with you.
Instead of thinking or saying, "You made me feel [emotion]," try starting your sentences with "I feel." This shift in language acknowledges your own role in your emotional experience and empowers you to take responsibility for your feelings.

Neuroscience Insight: The Internal Source of Happiness
The brain's emotional enters, such as the amygdala and prefrontal cortex, are deeply involved in how we experience happiness and satisfaction.
By taking responsibility for your own emotions and doing the inner work to cultivate happiness, you strengthen these neural pathways, leading to a more resilient and joyful mindset.

How I Found True Happiness in My Relationship with my wife Nadia:
For years, I held onto the belief that my partner was responsible for my happiness, that it was her job to fill my emotional gaps and make me feel complete. It's a common trap, thinking that our partner is our "other half" who must fix our problems and fill every void. But over time, I learned that this expectation is not only unfair but also damaging to the relationship.

Reality Check: Happiness Is an Inside Job
It wasn't Nadia's responsibility to make me happy. Neuroscience shows that our emotions stem from internal processes, not something that anyone else can control. Our brains, specifically the amygdala and prefrontal cortex, are where our emotions are processed, and it's within these neural networks that happiness is cultivated.

When I shifted my mindset to recognise that my happiness comes from within, not from someone else, everything changed. I stopped placing pressure on Nadia to be the source of my emotional fulfilment and started taking responsibility for my own happiness.

The Power of "I Feel" Instead of "You Made Me Feel"
One practical shift that helped me was changing the way I communicated. Instead of saying, "You made me feel upset," I began saying, "I feel upset." This shift may seem small, but it made a huge difference. By taking ownership of my feelings, I empowered myself and released Nadia from the unrealistic expectation of controlling my emotions.
This doesn't mean your partner can't support you. In fact, they can be an incredible source of comfort and joy. But the key is understanding that the emotional experience comes from within.

Neuroscience Insight: Rewiring the Brain for Happiness
By doing this inner work, you begin to strengthen the neural pathways in your brain that are connected to joy, love, and fulfilment. Consistently focusing on your own emotional health and happiness rewires your brain, making you more resilient and better equipped to experience deeper satisfaction in your relationship.
The truth is, once I took responsibility for my own happiness, our relationship grew stronger.
I stopped expecting Nadia to fill my emotional gaps and instead began appreciating her presence in my life without the weight of those unrealistic expectations.

The result? We now share a love that feels lighter, more joyful, more profound, and more fulfilling than ever before.

Happiness, I've learned, is an inside job. When you stop searching for it outside of yourself and take charge of your emotional experience, it opens the door to a much deeper, more meaningful connection with the one you love.

Journaling Prompts:
- **Own Your Emotions:** Write about a recent situation where you felt a strong emotion. Instead of focusing on what someone else did, explore what was happening inside you. What thoughts or beliefs contributed to your feelings?
- **Neuroscience Connection:** This practice encourages neural growth in the prefrontal cortex, which helps in emotional regulation and resilience.

- **Create a Happiness Plan:** Identify activities, practices, or habits that bring you joy and fulfilment independently of your partner. How can you incorporate more of these into your life?
- **Neuroscience Connection:** Regularly engaging in activities that promote happiness and self-care strengthens the brain's reward circuits, leading to a more positive and autonomous emotional state.

Conclusion: Building a Relationship on Truth and Effort
Debunking these myths allows us to build relationships on a foundation of truth, where both partners are whole individuals, responsible for their own happiness, yet fully committed to supporting each other's journey. By integrating these insights with daily journaling practices, you can create a relationship that is not just sustainable but deeply fulfiling.

Journaling Prompts:
- Reflect on Your Relationship Beliefs: Consider any other beliefs you hold about relationships. Are there other myths that might be influencing your expectations? How can you challenge these and replace them with more empowering beliefs?

By embracing these truths and doing the work, both individually and as a couple, you can create a relationship that thrives, where happiness is shared but not dependent, and where love is not a transaction but a mutual, continuous gift.

Here are several more journaling prompts designed to help you explore **Myth 4: "It's My Partner's Responsibility to Make Me Happy"** and take ownership of your emotional well-being:

Journaling Prompt:
- **In what ways have you expected your partner to make you happy?**

Reflect on past or present relationships where you may have placed the responsibility of your happiness on your partner. How did this affect the relationship dynamic?

- **How do you currently take responsibility for your own happiness?**

Write about the habits, thoughts, or actions that you practice to maintain your emotional well-being. What more could you do to ensure that your happiness comes from within?

- **What emotions have you blamed others for in the past?**

Think of moments where you said or thought, "You made me feel…" and explore how taking ownership of these feelings might change your outlook

- **What are some specific things that bring you joy, independent of anyone else?**

Identify activities, passions, or moments that make you happy without relying on external validation or the presence of a partner. How can you incorporate more of these into your life?

- **How would your relationships change if you stopped expecting your partner to "fix" your emotional problems?**

Visualise a relationship where you take full responsibility for your emotions. How would this shift affect both the conflicts and the positive experiences in your relationship?

- **When you feel upset, how do you process those emotions internally?**

Reflect on your emotional processing habits. Do you rely on others to help you regulate your emotions, or do you have self-soothing techniques that work for you?

- **What beliefs do you hold about your partner's role in your happiness?**

Examine any lingering beliefs that your partner should play a central role in making you happy. How can you reframe those beliefs to align with the reality that happiness is an inside job?

- **How can you communicate your emotional needs in a way that takes responsibility for your feelings?**

Practice using "I feel" statements in your journal. Write about a recent emotional situation and rephrase it from the perspective of owning your emotions, rather than placing them on someone else.

- **What is your definition of happiness, and how can you cultivate it within yourself?**
Explore your personal understanding of happiness. What does it mean to you, and what steps can you take to foster it in your life, independent of a partner?

- **What fears or insecurities arise when you think about being solely responsible for your happiness?**
Write about any discomfort or resistance you feel when faced with the idea that no one else can make you happy. What can you do to overcome these fears and empower yourself emotionally?

Journaling Instructions
When journaling, find a quiet, comfortable space where you won't be interrupted. Begin by setting an intention for your journaling session, focusing on self-awareness and reflection. Use these prompts to guide your writing, but allow yourself to explore whatever thoughts and feelings come up. Be honest with yourself, journaling is a personal process, and there's no need to censor your thoughts. Spend at least 10-15 minutes on each prompt, and if emotions arise, sit with them, process them, and explore how they inform your sense of self.

Consider revisiting your entries over time. As you develop more self-awareness, you may discover new insights or shift perspectives. This practice will help you rewire your brain to embrace wholeness and release the neediness that can lead to unhealthy attachment in relationships.

"Your feelings are your responsibility. The moment you stop outsourcing your happiness, you empower yourself and your relationship."

"When you stop seeking happiness from others, you begin to discover the infinite well of joy within yourself."

Chapter 15

Own Your Emotions:
Write about a recent situation where you felt a strong emotion. Instead of focusing on what someone else did, explore what was happening inside you. What thoughts or beliefs contributed to your feelings?

Chapter 16

Myth 5: "As Soon as You Have Children, Romance Begins to Die"

One of the most pervasive myths about relationships is the belief that, once children enter the picture, romance inevitably fades away. Couples often resign themselves to this notion, believing that passion and intimacy are destined to take a backseat to the demands of parenting. However, this myth is far from the truth. While parenthood undeniably changes your life, it doesn't mean the romantic spark between you and your partner has to fade.

The Reality: Your Partner is Still Your Lover
Becoming parents brings new challenges and responsibilities, but it doesn't erase the foundation of your relationship as lovers. Your partner was your lover before you had children, and they continue to be your lover now. While parenting may be demanding, it's vital to remember that nurturing your relationship is equally important for both your happiness and the well-being of your children.

Romance doesn't die after having children, it changes. Instead of spontaneous weekend getaways, romantic gestures may look like shared laughter over a morning cup of coffee or finding creative ways to connect during quiet moments. The key to sustaining romance is **prioritisation**. While your responsibilities have increased, it's essential to make space for your relationship. This might mean scheduling regular date nights, sharing affectionate moments, or simply talking about non-parenting-related topics.

It may require more effort and planning, but keeping romance alive is entirely possible if you prioritise it. Viewing each other not just as co-parents but as romantic partners helps maintain the
emotional and physical intimacy that bonds couples in the first place.

The Neuroscience of Sustaining Romance
The spark of romantic love doesn't just vanish with the arrival of children. The brain regions responsible for passion, such as the **ventral tegmental area (VTA)** and the **caudate nucleus**, are activated by feelings of motivation, reward, and connection. These are the same brain regions that were active when you first fell in love. By intentionally engaging in activities that foster romance, you can stimulate these areas, reinforcing your emotional bond and reigniting passion.

Romantic **love** engages the brain's dopamine system, which is responsible for pleasure and motivation. By planning date nights, giving each other **compliments**, or engaging in intimate conversations, you trigger dopamine release. This helps create feelings of **excitement and closeness**,
even amidst the responsibilities of raising children. Small, consistent gestures of love, such as holding hands or sharing a meaningful conversation, also activate the oxytocin system, the "bonding hormone," which deepens your connection and builds **trust**.

Prioritisation and Intention
The romance myth exists because we assume that when life becomes busier with children, there's simply no room left for passion. But the truth is, romance is about **intention**, not just time. Prioritising each other amid parenting tasks sends the message that your relationship remains central, not just as partners in raising children but as individuals who cherish and love each other.
Even short, focused moments of connection, like sharing a five-minute conversation or exchanging a heartfelt message, can have a profound impact on your relationship. It's about being **present and intentional** with your partner. Couples who make romance a consistent priority see greater satisfaction and emotional fulfilment.

Creating a New Normal for Romance After Kids
Instead of viewing children as the end of romance, you can see it as an opportunity to redefine intimacy and connection in new ways. Here are some key shifts in mindset that can help you maintain romance:

- **Set realistic expectations:** Accept that romance may not look the same as it did before children, but that doesn't mean it's gone. Acknowledge that time and energy are more limited, but creative solutions can keep the spark alive.

- **Communicate your needs:** Be open with your partner about how you can both maintain intimacy and connection. This can help you work together to keep your relationship strong while managing the challenges of parenthood.

- **Schedule quality time:** This may sound less romantic, but carving out intentional time for one another, even if it's once a week or once a month, is crucial. Regular date nights, walks, or time spent together without distractions can rejuvenate your bond.

- **Appreciate the little moments:** Grand gestures aren't necessary to maintain romance. Small actions like cuddling, a quick hug, or kind words can reinforce love in everyday life.

- **Keep intimacy alive:** Intimacy isn't just physical but emotional. Stay emotionally connected by sharing thoughts, dreams, and concerns with one another. This creates a deeper understanding and empathy, which strengthens the romantic connection.

Conclusion: Romance Isn't Dead, It Evolves
Romance doesn't have to die after children; it simply evolves.
By prioritising your relationship, communicating openly, and engaging in consistent acts of love, you can sustain and even enhance the romantic connection with your partner. Neuroscience shows that the brain's reward centres remain active in long-term relationships, especially when couples engage in intentional actions that stimulate love and passion.

While children can shift the dynamics of a relationship, they don't have to be the end of romance. Instead, they offer an opportunity to strengthen your bond, creating a partnership where love, passion, and parenting coexist beautifully.

Here are several journaling prompts to reflect on **Myth 5: "As Soon as You Have Children, Romance Begins to Die"** and explore how to maintain romance and connection in a relationship while navigating parenthood.

Journaling Prompts for Sustaining Romance After Children

- How do I currently prioritise my romantic relationship in the midst of parenting responsibilities?

Reflect on how much time and energy you are dedicating to your relationship as a couple. Are there areas where you feel disconnected or fulfilled?

- What were the small gestures and actions that made me feel connected to my partner before we had children?

Look back on the early days of your relationship. What were the things that kept the romantic spark alive? How can you reintroduce those moments now?

- How does my partner make me feel loved and appreciated today, and how do I show my love in return?

Consider the ways you and your partner currently express love. Are there small acts or changes that could help keep romance alive?

- What specific changes or efforts can I make to ensure that my partner feels valued and desired in our relationship, despite the demands of parenting?

Think about practical, actionable steps you can take to show your partner affection and prioritise intimacy.

- When was the last time I felt truly connected to my partner, and what contributed to that feeling?

Reflect on recent moments of connection. What worked, and how can you recreate that more often?

- How can I carve out time for romance and intimacy, even with the challenges of raising children?

Consider your current schedule. How can you intentionally create small moments of romance, and what adjustments are needed?

- In what ways can I communicate more openly with my partner about our needs for intimacy and connection?

Journaling about how to improve communication can help you be more intentional and direct with your partner about what you both need to sustain romance.

- What new ways can I and my partner connect romantically that fit into our current lifestyle as parents?

Explore creative solutions for maintaining romance, such as date nights at home, surprise gestures, or even small moments of affection.

- How does the idea of evolving romance, rather than losing it, resonate with me?

Reflect on how your perception of romance has changed since becoming a parent, and how you can embrace this new phase of your relationship.

- How do I balance the demands of parenting with the emotional and physical needs of my partner and myself?

Think about how you balance caregiving with nurturing your romantic connection. What are some ways you can improve or make changes to ensure both thrive?

Journaling Instructions:

Set aside 10-15 minutes for each prompt. Begin by free-writing your thoughts without editing or judgment. Let your ideas flow naturally.
Be honest and vulnerable with your answers. The goal of these prompts is to reflect deeply and generate insights into your relationship.
Review your responses after writing. Highlight any patterns, realisations, or actions that you can implement to enhance your relationship.
Use this journaling practice regularly. Reflecting on your romantic connection amidst parenting responsibilities can help you stay intentional and proactive about keeping your love alive.

"Love after children is an intentional act; it requires effort, but the reward is a relationship that grows deeper and stronger over time."

"True intimacy thrives when you prioritise each other, even amidst the demands of raising children."

Chapter 16

How do I currently prioritise my romantic relationship in the midst of parenting responsibilities?
Reflect on how much time and energy you are dedicating to your relationship as a couple. Are there areas where you feel disconnected or fulfilled?

Chapter 17

"Your Relationship with Yourself"

The Power of Self-Relationship in Romantic Bonds
A relationship with another person is often a reflection of the relationship you have with yourself. Neuroscience sheds light on why this is so critical. If you struggle with self-love, self-confidence, or personal happiness, it is not just an emotional issue but a neurobiological one. The brain's wiring directly affects your ability to connect with others, build trust, and sustain healthy relationships. No matter how much love or validation your partner provides, if the underlying neural circuits tied to self-worth are underdeveloped or activated by insecurity, it will be nearly impossible to truly feel fulfilled.

Neuroscience highlights that our self-perception is closely linked to the brain's **default mode network (DMN)**, a network of brain regions involved in self-referential thinking. When this network is overly focused on negative self-beliefs, it can lead to a loop of self-doubt, insecurity, and unhappiness. If you're constantly trapped in this loop, you'll find yourself seeking external validation from your partner or other sources, but this will only provide temporary relief.
You'll continuously need external reassurance, which can put undue pressure on your relationship and prevent you from fully being present or contributing positively.

The Role of Dopamine and Self-Worth
Neuroscientific studies suggest that dopamine, the brain's "reward" chemical, plays a major role in our sense of accomplishment, motivation, and self-esteem. When you engage in activities that promote self-growth, such as achieving personal goals, learning new things, or nurturing yourself, dopamine is released, making you feel satisfied and confident. This chemical boost enhances your internal sense of worth, reinforcing positive neural pathways that allow you to feel fulfilled from within, rather than needing constant external validation.

Conversely, if you neglect personal growth or focus on external sources of happiness (like depending on your partner for validation), your brain becomes accustomed to receiving dopamine from external triggers.

This can create a cycle of dependency where you are always looking to your partner or others to make you feel happy, resulting in a fragile emotional foundation. When the external stimuli are gone or diminished, feelings of emptiness can take over.

Emotional Regulation and the Prefrontal Cortex
When you consistently work on self-growth, you strengthen the **prefrontal cortex**, the part of the brain responsible for decision-making, emotional regulation, and impulse control. A well-developed prefrontal cortex helps you navigate emotional situations with greater clarity and patience, allowing you to respond to challenges in your relationship from a calm, centred space.

This neurobiological foundation helps you avoid reactive patterns, such as blaming or withdrawing, that can undermine a relationship.
Moreover, the brain's **limbic system**, especially the **amygdala**, is responsible for processing emotions like fear, anger, and anxiety. In individuals who lack self-confidence or struggle with self-love, the amygdala tends to be hyperactive, making them more prone to emotional reactivity.

This can lead to unhealthy patterns like jealousy, neediness, or emotional outbursts, which place strain on the relationship. Regular self-care, mindfulness, and personal growth activities help to calm the amygdala's response, promoting emotional resilience and stability.

Self-Growth and Attachment Styles
From an attachment theory perspective, neuroscience shows that your relationship with yourself is deeply tied to your attachment style. For example, if you have an anxious attachment style, you are likely wired to crave constant reassurance and may fear abandonment. This pattern stems from early childhood experiences but can be rewired through intentional self-development.

Research shows that neuroplasticity, the brain's ability to form new connections, allows individuals to change their attachment patterns by consistently engaging in behaviours that build self-assurance and emotional independence. Developing a secure attachment within yourself enables you to bring more security into your relationship.

Mirror Neurons and Your Partner's Experience
Neuroscientists have also identified **mirror neurons**, specialised brain cells that help us empathise with others by "mirroring" their emotional state. When you radiate self-confidence and self-love, your partner's mirror neurons will pick up on this positive emotional energy, making them feel more comfortable, loved, and secure in the relationship. Conversely, if you struggle with self-worth, your partner may unconsciously absorb your insecurity, leading to a more anxious or turbulent emotional atmosphere in the relationship.

Building a Fulfilling Self-Relationship
To truly contribute to your relationship, it is essential to focus on building a strong, positive relationship with yourself. This includes:

- **Engaging in Personal Growth Activities**: Whether it's learning a new skill, pursuing a passion, or working toward a personal goal, personal achievements trigger dopamine production in the brain. This fosters an intrinsic sense of accomplishment, boosting self-worth.
- **Mindfulness and Meditation**: These practices help calm the amygdala and strengthen the prefrontal cortex, leading to better emotional regulation and less dependency on external validation. Neuroscience shows that regular mindfulness practices can actually rewire the brain for greater emotional resilience.
- **Developing Emotional Awareness**: Journaling, therapy, or introspective practices that help you become more aware of your emotional patterns allow you to reframe negative self-talk.By transforming "I am not enough" into "I am worthy," you can rewire the default mode network to create a more positive self-perception.
- **Practicing Self-Compassion**: Research indicates that self-compassion activates the brain's reward system in much the same way that external validation does. By being kind to yourself, especially during challenging moments, you reduce emotional reactivity and foster internal stability.

By understanding how the brain influences your emotional and relational health, you can begin to work on the inner aspects of yourself that make for a more fulfilling partnership. When you build a strong foundation of self-love, you become less reliant on your partner for emotional support, which in turn creates space for a healthier, more balanced, and enriching relationship.

Journaling Instructions
To strengthen your relationship with yourself and apply neuroscience-based insights, set aside 10-15 minutes daily for journaling. Each prompt is designed to help you reflect on self-love, emotional regulation, and personal growth, contributing positively to both your personal well-being and your relationship. When answering these prompts, aim for honesty, curiosity, and self- compassion. Don't rush the process, let your thoughts flow naturally, and explore any emotions or insights that arise.

Journaling Prompts

- **Self-Love Reflection:**
  - Prompt: "In what ways do I currently show love and kindness to myself? Where in my life could I be more compassionate toward myself?"
  - Neuroscience Insight: Activating self-compassion can stimulate the brain's reward system. Reflect on how you can nurture these pathways with daily acts of self-love.

- **Emotional Triggers Exploration:**
  - Prompt: "What situations or interactions in my life tend to trigger negative self-talk? How can I reframe these thoughts with self-empowering beliefs?"
  - Neuroscience Insight: Reframing negative self-talk rewires the default mode network in your brain, helping you build a healthier self-perception.

- **Growth Mindset:**
  - Prompt: "What areas of personal growth excite me right now? How does pursuing these interests make me feel more fulfilled and self-confident?"
  - Neuroscience Insight: Dopamine is released when you engage in personal growth, fostering motivation and a stronger sense of self-worth.

- **Emotional Regulation in Relationships:**
  - Prompt: "How do I typically react when I feel emotionally triggered in my relationship? What can I do to bring more mindfulness into those moments?"
  - Neuroscience Insight: Calming your brain's amygdala with mindful breathing and reflection helps build emotional resilience and improves relationship dynamics.

- **Inner Self-Dialogue:**
  - Prompt: "What is the tone of my inner self-dialogue? How can I replace harsh self-criticism with words that reflect my intrinsic worth?"
  - Neuroscience Insight: Kind inner dialogue activates positive neural pathways, reducing emotional reactivity and increasing your sense of self-compassion.

- **Abundance and Contentment:**
  - Prompt: "What aspects of my life am I truly grateful for right now? How can I shift my focus from what I 'need' externally to the abundance I already have?"
  - Neuroscience Insight: Focusing on gratitude triggers dopamine release and reinforces neural pathways associated with fulfilment and contentment.

- **Self-Validation vs. External Validation:**
  - Prompt: "In what areas of my life do I seek validation from others? How can I cultivate a stronger sense of self-worth from within?"
  - Neuroscience Insight: When you rely on external validation, you create temporary dopamine spikes. Building self-validation strengthens intrinsic emotional stability.

- Strengthening Self-Belief:
    - Prompt: "What limiting beliefs do I hold about myself? How can I challenge these beliefs and reinforce the idea that I am capable and worthy?"
    - Neuroscience Insight: Challenging and replacing limiting beliefs can rewire the brain, leading to greater confidence and motivation.

- Maintaining Individuality in Relationships:
    - Prompt: "How do I maintain my individuality in my relationship? In what ways can I continue to nurture my own passions and goals?"
    - Neuroscience Insight: Maintaining individuality strengthens the brain's motivational pathways, contributing to a healthier, more balanced relationship dynamic.

- Mirror Neurons and Positive Energy:
    - Prompt: "How does my mood and energy influence my partner's emotional state? How can I consciously project more positive energy in my relationship?"
    - Neuroscience Insight: Mirror neurons in the brain help partners unconsciously reflect each other's emotions, which means your positive energy can foster deeper connection.

Tips for Effective Journaling
- Write Freely: Don't censor or overthink your responses. Allow your thoughts to flow naturally without judgment.
- Revisit & Reflect: Periodically review your journal entries to notice patterns and personal growth.
- Stay Consistent: Make journaling a regular habit to reinforce the neural pathways related to self-love, emotional regulation, and growth.
- Practice Gratitude: Conclude each journaling session by noting something you're grateful for, reinforcing positive mental patterns.

Through regular journaling and self-reflection, you can harness the power of neuroscience to deepen your self-relationship and, in turn, bring more positivity and balance to your romantic relationships.

Chapter 17

Self-Love Reflection:
"In what ways do I currently show love and kindness to myself? Where in my life could I be more compassionate toward myself?"

Chapter 18
Confidence vs. Desperation

Expanding on this concept from a neuroscience perspective, the reason people are typically attracted to individuals who exude confidence rather than desperation lies in the intricate workings of the brain and its interpretation of social signals. Our brains are finely tuned to pick up on cues related to confidence, self-worth, and emotional security, all of which have evolutionary roots and influence attraction.

The Science of Confidence vs. Desperation
Desperation, from a neurological perspective, is associated with anxiety and uncertainty, which triggers the release of stress hormones like cortisol. When someone is desperate or overly clingy, their brain is in a heightened state of stress or neediness, which can negatively affect their body language, tone of voice, and even decision-making. These signs of insecurity are picked up by others, who instinctively feel that the desperate individual may not be emotionally stable or self-assured, leading to a natural aversion.

In contrast, people who are confident and relaxed signal safety and emotional stability. This activates the reward system in the brain, which involves the release of dopamine (the "feel-good" hormone) and oxytocin (the bonding hormone). These neurochemicals are associated with pleasure, trust, and connection, which makes confident individuals more attractive. The brain is drawn to environments and people that offer a sense of security and positive emotional experiences, making confidence a key trait in romantic attraction.

Mirror Neurons and Social Interaction
Neuroscience also points to the role of mirror neurons, which are brain cells that fire both when we perform an action and when we observe someone else performing the same action. These neurons allow us to empathise with others and understand their emotions and intentions. When we encounter someone who exudes confidence and self-assurance, our mirror neurons help us feel a sense of calm and stability. We tend to mirror that energy, feeling more at ease and positive around them.

On the other hand, when we are around someone who is desperate or anxious, our mirror neurons pick up on those signals as well, potentially triggering our own stress response. This is why people often feel uncomfortable or repelled by individuals who are overly needy or clingy. The brain, seeking to avoid stress and negativity, gravitates toward individuals who project self-sufficiency and emotional balance.

Evolutionary Psychology: Attraction to Stability
From an evolutionary standpoint, confidence is associated with survival and reproductive success. In our ancestral past, individuals who were emotionally stable, self-reliant, and confident were better able to secure resources, protect themselves and their families, and navigate social hierarchies. As a result, these traits became highly desirable in potential mates. Desperation, on the other hand, may signal weakness, insecurity, or a lack of resources, which are less attractive traits from an evolutionary perspective.

When someone displays confidence, it indicates that they are emotionally grounded, independent, and capable of handling challenges. These are all qualities that increase the chances of a successful partnership, making such individuals more appealing. Desperation, on the other hand, suggests that a person is seeking external validation or support to fill an internal void, which can be perceived as a liability in a relationship.

The Role of Attachment Styles
Neuroscience also ties into attachment theory, which helps explain why certain individuals may appear more desperate or clingy in relationships. People with anxious attachment styles, for example, are more likely to experience heightened activity in brain areas associated with fear and emotional regulation, such as the amygdala. This can make them more prone to clinginess and emotional dependency on others for reassurance. On the other hand, individuals with secure attachment styles tend to have more balanced brain activity in response to stress and emotional challenges, allowing them to maintain a sense of independence and confidence in relationships.

Conclusion: Confidence and Neural Wiring
Attraction is not just about looks or charm, it's deeply rooted in how our brains interpret emotional cues. Confidence, emotional stability, and self-assuredness create a neurochemical and psychological response that makes people more appealing, while desperation activates stress responses that lead to avoidance. By understanding the neuroscience behind attraction, it becomes clear that cultivating a sense of self-worth, emotional independence, and calm is key to attracting positive relationships.

In summary, the science behind why people are attracted to confident individuals is rooted in the brain's drive to seek out safety, stability, and positive experiences. Confidence activates reward systems in the brain, while desperation triggers stress responses, making it clear why self-assuredness is so magnetic in human interactions.

Journaling Instructions
Journaling is a powerful tool for self-reflection, awareness, and emotional growth. To effectively journal based on the concepts outlined above, follow these instructions:
1. **Set the Mood:** Find a quiet space where you can be uninterrupted for at least 15–20 minutes. You may want to light a candle or play some soft music to set a calming environment.
2. **Stay Open:** Approach your journaling session with curiosity and openness. There is no right or wrong answer; allow your thoughts and emotions to flow freely.
3. **Write Consistently:** Write every day or several times a week to build the habit of self-reflection. The more consistently you engage in journaling, the more insight you will gain.
4. **Focus on Feelings:** As you answer these prompts, focus not just on the events or actions, but also on your emotions and the patterns in your thinking. This will help you uncover deeper truths about yourself.
5. **Be Honest:** Write without judgment, allowing yourself to explore your true thoughts and feelings. Honesty with yourself is crucial for growth.

Journaling Prompts

- How do I typically feel about myself in romantic relationships?
    - Reflect on your emotional state when interacting with partners. Do you feel confident, or do you find yourself seeking validation? Explore how your self-perception impacts your relationships.

- When was the last time I felt desperate for love, validation, or attention?
    - Describe the situation, your feelings, and how you responded. Reflect on how these feelings of desperation may have affected your interactions with others.

- How do I define confidence, and how does it show up in my relationships?
    - Consider what confidence looks like to you. Do you naturally embody this in your interactions, or do you find yourself struggling to maintain a sense of self-assurance?

- What are some behaviours or thoughts that I exhibit when I feel insecure in a relationship?
    - Identify the ways in which you act or think when insecurity creeps in. Be specific about how this affects your behaviour towards your partner.

- In what areas of my life do I rely on external validation, and how can I cultivate internal validation?
    - Reflect on where in your life you seek approval from others. Consider practical steps you can take to develop a stronger sense of self-worth without relying on external sources.

- How does my current attachment style impact my relationships, and what steps can I take to foster a more secure attachment?
    - Explore your attachment style (anxious, avoidant, or secure) and how it shapes your relationships. Reflect on ways you can develop a more secure attachment by working on your inner self.

- What small actions can I take to increase my emotional independence in relationships?
    - List a few daily practices or mindsets that could help you feel more grounded in yourself. For example, practicing gratitude, self-care, or pursuing personal goals.
- How do I react to rejection or criticism in relationships?
    - Consider how you handle these negative experiences. Do you take it personally, or can you stay grounded? Reflect on how you can strengthen your resilience to external opinions.
- What steps can I take to change my inner dialogue from "I can't" to "I can"?
    - Examine your current self-talk. When do you tell yourself that you're not capable? How can you reframe these thoughts in a positive, affirming way?
- What examples from my own life show that confidence leads to better outcomes?
    - Think of a time when you felt confident and how that situation unfolded. Contrast it with times when you were insecure, and reflect on the differences in outcome.

These journaling prompts are designed to help you explore the impact of self-confidence, emotional independence, and internal validation on your relationships. As you journal, focus on uncovering deeper emotional patterns and identifying practical steps to build a more confident and secure version of yourself.

"True confidence comes from knowing that your value doesn't depend on others' validation, but on your own belief in yourself."

Chapter 18

How do I typically feel about myself in romantic relationships?
Reflect on your emotional state when interacting with partners. Do you feel confident, or do you find yourself seeking validation? Explore how your self- perception impacts your relationships.

Chapter 19

Joyful and Fulfilling Relationship

The Key to a Joyful and Fulfilling Relationship
A truly successful and joyful relationship is one that allows you to access the deepest, most authentic parts of yourself. It's not about always looking good together or maintaining a facade of constant happiness. Instead, the most fulfilling relationships are those where you can tap into your vulnerability, courage, and engage in deep truth-telling.

The Power of True Intimacy
True intimacy is about sharing the most vulnerable aspects of yourself with your partner and trusting them to create a safe, judgment-free space for you. This level of safety is essential for deep connection, but it can also be intimidating to seek or offer. However, when you put everything on the table with respect for both yourself and your partner, you build greater trust, love, and a stronger bond.

The Neuroscience of Vulnerability and Connection
Neuroscience shows that when we engage in vulnerable and honest communication, we activate the brain's reward circuits, particularly those associated with trust and bonding. Oxytocin, often called the "love hormone," is released during moments of vulnerability and connection, fostering a sense of security and closeness with our partner.

Journaling Prompts:
- **Embrace Vulnerability:** Reflect on a time when you felt truly vulnerable with your partner. What did you share, and how did they respond? How did this experience impact your relationship?

Neuroscience Connection: Recognising and processing these moments can strengthen neural pathways associated with trust and emotional intimacy.

- **Build Safety:** Consider ways you can create a safe space for your partner to share their vulnerabilities. What actions or words can help build this trust?

Neuroscience Connection: Creating a safe environment for emotional expression can enhance the brain's oxytocin levels, reinforcing the bond between partners.

Embracing Wholeness in Relationships
When we accept that our partners are not here to complete us, we open the door to the happiness we truly desire. This shift in perspective allows us to see that wholeness isn't about achieving perfection but rather about embracing our imperfections and those of our partner. It's about connecting to our deepest values and welcoming profound love, intimacy, and relationship bliss.

Journaling Prompts:
- **Redefine Perfection:** Reflect on areas where you've held yourself or your partner to unrealistic standards. How can you shift your mindset to embrace imperfections and see them as part of the journey to deeper connection?

Neuroscience Connection: Letting go of perfectionism can reduce stress and activate the brain's compassion circuits, fostering more understanding and empathy in your relationship.

- **Align with Values:** Identify your core values and consider whether your current relationship choices align with these values. How can you bring more of your true self into your relationship?

Neuroscience Connection: Aligning your actions with your values can enhance your sense of authenticity and well-being, positively impacting your relationship dynamics.

Journaling Instructions

On the following pages, take the time to answer the questions from the journaling prompts provided in this chapter. These prompts are designed to help you reflect deeply on your relationship, uncover new insights, and foster greater understanding between you and your partner.

Feel free to use several additional blank pages in your notebook, in addition to the ones provided in this book. These extra pages will allow you to dive deeper into the journaling prompts and exercises, giving you space to explore your thoughts and feelings more fully. Whether you're working through complex emotions, visualising your ideal relationship, or reflecting on past experiences, having extra space will give you the freedom to express yourself without limitations. Take your time, and let your reflections flow naturally.

Chapter 19

Embrace Vulnerability: *Reflect on a time when you felt truly vulnerable with your partner. What did you share, and how did they respond? How did this experience impact your relationship?*

Chapter 20
Avoiding Convenience and Embracing Authenticity

Many people enter relationships out of convenience or fear of being alone, rather than from a place of true alignment with their values and desires. It's important to gain clarity on what you genuinely want in a relationship and partner, and to be willing to grow and change to attract this kind of connection.

This isn't just about making a checklist of superficial qualities, like physical appearance or shared hobbies, but about delving deeper into your belief systems. Are your relationship choices aligned with what you truly care about? Or are you falling for partners who merely meet the superficial, societally approved criteria?

Learning from Every Relationship
Every relationship, whether it lasts or not, has the potential to teach us something valuable about ourselves and our desires. Just because a relationship ends doesn't mean it wasn't successful or didn't serve a meaningful purpose. Often, relationships that don't work out help us get closer to understanding who we truly are and what we need to feel fulfilled.

The Neuroscience of Growth Through Relationships
Each relationship, even those that end, contributes to our brain's understanding of connection, attachment, and personal growth. By processing and learning from these experiences, we can rewire our brain for better future relationships.

Journaling Prompts:
- **Clarify Your Priorities:** Write about the qualities you truly value in a partner and a relationship. How do these align with your deeper needs and desires?

Neuroscience Connection: Clarifying your values can engage the brain's executive functions, helping you make decisions that align with your authentic self.

- **Reflect on Past Relationships:** Think about previous relationships that have ended. What did you learn about yourself and your needs? How can these insights guide your future relationship choices?

Neuroscience Connection: Reflecting on past experiences can strengthen neural connections related to self-awareness, aiding in personal growth and better relationship decisions.

Journaling Prompts:
- **See the Blessings:** Reflect on a past relationship that ended. What lessons did you learn, and how have these shaped your understanding of love and connection?

Neuroscience Connection: Recognising the positive outcomes of past relationships can activate the brain's reward centres, reinforcing a growth-oriented mindset.

- **Envision Future Growth:** Consider how you can apply the lessons from past relationships to your current or future ones. What personal growth steps are you willing to take to contribute more meaningfully to your relationship?

Neuroscience Connection: Setting goals for personal and relational growth can engage the brain's planning and reward systems, enhancing motivation and fulfilment.

Conclusion: Cultivating a Relationship Full of Joy and Fulfilment

A relationship that allows for deep vulnerability, mutual growth, and the embracing of imperfections is one that can bring profound joy and fulfilment. By focusing on your own growth, aligning your relationship choices with your core values, and learning from every relationship experience, you can build a partnership that thrives on authenticity and love.

Final Journaling Prompt:
Commit to Growth: Write a commitment to yourself and your relationship. How will you continue to grow, embrace vulnerability, and align your relationship with your true values?

Through these reflections and practices, you can cultivate a relationship that is resilient, authentic, and deeply fulfilling, leading to lasting joy and profound love.

Journaling Instructions

On the following pages, take the time to answer the questions from the journaling prompts provided in this chapter. These prompts are designed to help you reflect deeply on your relationship, uncover new insights, and foster greater understanding between you and your partner.

Use the journaling pages within this book to guide your reflections at the end of each chapter, and pair this with a separate notebook to journal twice daily. Morning journaling helps set your intentions, clarify your goals, and align your mindset for the day ahead. It activates the brain's prefrontal cortex, enhancing focus and decision-making. Evening journaling, on the other hand, allows for reflection on the day's experiences, processing emotions, and reinforcing positive neural pathways as you sleep.
By combining both practices, you're maximising the brain's ability to rewire itself toward emotional healing, self-awareness, and long-term well-being.

Chapter 20

Clarify Your Priorities: *Write about the qualities you truly value in a partner and a relationship. How do these align with your deeper needs and desires?*

Chapter 21

Myth Seven: Being Miserable and Arguing All the Time is Normal

It's a widespread misconception that constant arguing and unhappiness are simply a part of any relationship. Many people believe that frequent conflicts and dissatisfaction are unavoidable, and that they signify a normal, albeit challenging, relationship. This belief can be so pervasive that even experienced relationship coaches and therapists sometimes accept it as a given.

In my work with clients, I've found that this notion is deeply ingrained. Some argue that conflict is natural and can even be beneficial if approached with love and compassion. They suggest that arguing helps communicate frustrations and needs, and that it's possible to have constructive conflicts. However, this perspective overlooks the fact that constant arguing and unhappiness are neither normal nor healthy.

The idea that daily disputes and persistent dissatisfaction are a standard part of relationships is misguided. True, disagreements are a natural part of any relationship, but they should not define your everyday experience. An environment dominated by constant conflict is not conducive to a healthy, thriving relationship.

A healthy relationship should be marked by mutual respect, understanding, and support. While occasional disagreements are normal, they should be handled in a way that strengthens rather than weakens the bond between partners.

Journaling Prompts:

- **Reflect on Conflict Patterns:** Reflect on recent arguments or conflicts in your relationship. What patterns or triggers do you notice? How might these patterns be affecting your overall happiness and relationship health?

- **Healthy Communication Practices:** Describe a recent disagreement where communication was particularly effective or ineffective. What strategies or approaches helped or hindered the resolution? How can you apply these insights to improve communication in future conflicts?

- **Identifying Core Issues:** Think about the recurring issues or themes in your arguments. Are there underlying problems or unmet needs that are consistently driving these conflicts? How can addressing these core issues improve your relationship?

- **Vision of a Healthy Relationship:** Envision what a healthy, conflict-free relationship looks like to you. What are the key elements that contribute to this vision? How can you and your partner work together to move towards this ideal?

- **Self-Reflection on Conflict Management:** How do you typically handle conflicts or disagreements? Reflect on your approach and its impact on your relationship. Are there changes you can make to handle conflicts more constructively?

- **Neuroscience of Stress and Conflict:** Research suggests that chronic conflict can trigger stress responses in the brain, affecting both mental and physical health. How might reducing unnecessary conflicts benefit your overall well-being and relationship dynamics?

- **Creating a Conflict-Resolution Plan:** Develop a plan for resolving conflicts in a healthy manner. What steps can you take to ensure that disagreements are addressed constructively and without escalating into arguments?

- **Role of Empathy in Conflict:** Reflect on a time when empathy played a key role in resolving a conflict. How did understanding your partner's perspective help in finding a resolution? How can you incorporate more empathy into your conflict resolution strategies?

- **Balancing Conflict and Connection:** Write about how you can balance addressing conflicts with nurturing positive aspects of your relationship. How can you ensure that the focus remains on maintaining a strong, loving connection despite disagreements?

- **Evaluating Relationship Health:** Assess your relationship's overall health and satisfaction. How often do you feel unhappy or engaged in arguments compared to feeling content and connected? What changes can you make to enhance the positive aspects of your relationship?

By recognising that constant arguing and unhappiness are not normal or acceptable, you can shift towards creating a relationship that is healthier, more supportive, and fulfilling. Emphasising positive communication and conflict resolution can transform your relationship into one marked by mutual respect and understanding.

Journaling Instructions

On the following pages, and additionally in your notebook, take the time to answer the questions from the journaling prompts provided in this chapter. These prompts are designed to help you reflect deeply on your relationship, uncover new insights, and foster greater understanding between you and your partner.

Use the journaling pages within this book to guide your reflections at the end of each chapter, and pair this with a separate notebook to journal twice daily. Morning journaling helps set your intentions, clarify your goals, and align your mindset for the day ahead. It activates the brain's prefrontal cortex, enhancing focus and decision-making. Evening journaling, on the other hand, allows for reflection on the day's experiences, processing emotions, and reinforcing positive neural pathways as you sleep.

By combining both practices, you're maximising the brain's ability to rewire itself toward emotional healing, self-awareness, and long-term well-being.

Chapter 21

Reflect on Conflict Patterns: *Reflect on recent arguments or conflicts in your relationship. What patterns or triggers do you notice? How might these patterns be affecting your overall happiness and relationship health?*

Chapter 22

Myth Seven part 2: Constant Fighting and Arguing Are Normal in Relationships

Many so-called relationship experts and self-help books claim that frequent fighting and arguing are just part of a normal, healthy relationship. They suggest that it's not the frequency of the arguments but the manner in which you fight, "fighting fair", that matters. I strongly disagree with this viewpoint.

In my experience, no amount of "fighting fair" can justify or normalise constant arguments and unhappiness in a relationship. I believe in striving for a relationship where disagreements are rare, and the focus is on mutual respect and joy.

I want a relationship where my partner and I are deeply connected, continuously falling in love with each other, and experiencing what feels like a perpetual honeymoon. A relationship where every day is an opportunity to express love, appreciation, and respect. I want to feel that our bond grows stronger each day and that we both thrive in an environment of profound happiness and fulfilment.

Journaling Prompts to Enhance Your Relationship:

- **Evaluating Dispute Frequency:** Reflect on the frequency and nature of conflicts in your relationship. How often do you argue, and what are the typical triggers? How does this frequency affect your overall satisfaction and well-being?

- **Exploring Alternative Conflict Solutions:** Brainstorm and document alternative ways to address disagreements without resorting to conflict. What strategies could you employ to resolve issues in a more constructive and harmonious way?

- **Understanding Emotional Responses:** Explore how constant arguing affects your brain's stress response. How do chronic conflicts impact your emotional and physical health? What steps can you take to minimise these stress responses?

- **Imagining a Conflict-Free Relationship:** Visualise what your ideal relationship looks like without frequent arguments. What are the key characteristics of this relationship? How can you work towards creating this kind of dynamic with your partner?

- **Enhancing Emotional Intimacy:** Reflect on how emotional intimacy and vulnerability contribute to your relationship's overall health. How can deepening your emotional connection help reduce conflicts and increase mutual understanding?

- **Strategies for Positive Communication:** Consider ways to enhance your communication skills to avoid misunderstandings and conflicts. What methods can you adopt to ensure that your conversations are productive and nurturing rather than contentious?

- **Assessing Your Relationship Goals:** Write about your personal goals for your relationship. How can focusing on these goals shift the dynamics away from frequent arguments and towards a more loving and supportive partnership?

- **Identifying and Addressing Triggers:** Identify specific triggers that lead to arguments. How can you and your partner address these triggers constructively? What preventative measures can you put in place?

- **Building a Culture of Appreciation:** Document ways to express appreciation and gratitude in your relationship regularly. How can cultivating a habit of positive reinforcement influence your relationship dynamics and reduce conflicts?

- **Creating a Vision for a Thriving Relationship:** Develop a detailed vision for a thriving relationship where both partners feel loved and fulfilled. What daily practices and attitudes can support this vision and ensure that arguments are minimised?

By focusing on nurturing positive interactions and fostering a deeper emotional connection, you can transform your relationship into one characterised by joy, love, and mutual respect.
Shifting away from a mindset that normalises constant fighting allows for a more fulfilling and harmonious partnership.

Journaling Instructions
On the following pages, take the time to answer the questions from the journaling prompts provided in this chapter. These prompts are designed to help you reflect deeply on your relationship, uncover new insights, and foster greater understanding between you and your partner.

Use the journaling pages within this book to guide your reflections at the end of each chapter, and pair this with a separate notebook to journal twice daily. Morning journaling helps set your intentions, clarify your goals, and align your mindset for the day ahead. It activates the brain's prefrontal cortex, enhancing focus and decision-making. Evening journaling, on the other hand, allows for reflection on the day's experiences, processing emotions, and reinforcing positive neural pathways as you sleep.
By combining both practices, you're maximising the brain's ability to rewire itself toward emotional healing, self-awareness, and long-term well-being.

"Arguing too often is not love; it's two people battling their unresolved issues."

"A relationship based on love should feel like a safe space, not a battlefield."

"When you fight more than you laugh, it's time to rethink your idea of a healthy relationship."

"When love is at the core of your relationship, disagreements are handled with care, not with combat."

Chapter 22

Evaluating Dispute Frequency: *Reflect on the frequency and nature of conflicts in your relationship. How often do you argue, and what are the typical triggers? How does this frequency affect your overall satisfaction and well-being?*

Chapter 23

Transforming Conflict into Connection: A Path to Lasting Relationship Bliss

When I tell my clients that improving their relationship requires consistent effort, it can seem daunting at first. However, much like developing any new habit, this process becomes effortless over time. The key is to engage daily with genuine contributions from the heart. The road to a deep, meaningful relationship full of love, fulfilment, and genuine bliss lies in positive, daily, and consistent efforts, which become effortless over time due to neuroplasticity and the formation of new, positive neural pathways in the brain.

If you find yourself frequently arguing with your partner, it may signal unresolved emotions and internal discomfort. Early in the relationship, your heart was wide open, and you embraced vulnerability effortlessly. But over time, as conflicts arise, you may start to feel insulted or attacked, leading you to close off emotionally. What once was a loving partnership may start to feel like a battleground, where each argument becomes a match with defensive tactics, leading to increased frustration and a feeling of hopelessness.

To move beyond this cycle and rekindle the connection you once had, consider these journaling prompts based on neuroscience to help you make the best of your relationship and
heal any rifts:

Journaling Prompts Based on Neuroscience:

- **Uncovering Hidden Emotions:**
    - Reflect on the unresolved emotions that may be fuelling your arguments. What feelings are you holding onto that might be causing discomfort or conflict? How can acknowledging these emotions help in reducing conflicts?

- **Understanding Emotional Triggers:**
  - Identify common triggers that lead to arguments. How do these triggers affect your emotional state? What steps can you take to address these triggers proactively?

- **Exploring Vulnerability:**
  - Think about how you felt when you first opened your heart to your partner. How has this sense of vulnerability changed over time? What can you do to reintroduce this openness into your relationship?

- **Assessing Communication Patterns:**
  - Analyse your communication patterns during conflicts. How do you typically respond to arguments? How can you alter your approach to promote more constructive and empathetic communication?

- **Recognising Emotional Conditioning:**
  - Reflect on how frequent arguments might have conditioned you to be on constant alert. How does this heightened state of vigilance affect your relationship? What practices can help you relax and reduce this tension?

- **Reconnecting with Love:**
  - Write about the qualities you love in your partner and the initial reasons why you fell in love. How can reconnecting with these positive aspects help shift your focus away from conflicts?

- **Developing Compassionate Responses:**
  - Explore ways to respond to conflicts with compassion rather than defensiveness. What new strategies can you implement to handle disagreements with greater understanding and empathy?

- **Evaluating the Impact of Arguments:**
  - Consider the impact of frequent arguments on your overall relationship satisfaction. How do these arguments affect your emotional well-being and your partner's? What changes can you make to reduce this impact?

- **Envisioning a Harmonious Relationship:**
  - Visualise your ideal relationship where conflicts are rare and resolution comes easily. What steps can you take to create this vision in your current relationship?

- **Commitment to Positive Change:**
  - Write about your commitment to positive changes in your relationship. How can you and your partner work together to foster a more harmonious and fulfilling partnership?

By exploring these prompts, you can gain insight into your emotional responses and communication patterns, allowing you to address conflicts more effectively and nurture a relationship where love and connection thrive.

Journaling Instructions

On the following pages, take the time to answer the questions from the journaling prompts provided in this chapter. These prompts are designed to help you reflect deeply on your relationship, uncover new insights, and foster greater understanding between you and your partner.

Use the journaling pages within this book to guide your reflections at the end of each chapter, and pair this with a separate notebook to journal twice daily. Morning journaling helps set your intentions, clarify your goals, and align your mindset for the day ahead. It activates the brain's prefrontal cortex, enhancing focus and decision-making. Evening journaling, on the other hand, allows for reflection on the day's experiences, processing emotions, and reinforcing positive neural pathways as you sleep.

By combining both practices, you're maximising the brain's ability to rewire itself toward emotional healing, self-awareness, and long-term well-being.

Chapter 23

Uncovering Hidden Emotions: *Reflect on the unresolved emotions that may be fuelling your arguments. What feelings are you holding onto that might be causing discomfort or conflict? How can acknowledging these emotions help in reducing conflicts?*

Chapter 24

Breaking the Cycle of Conflict: Reclaiming Your Heart and Happiness

You may find yourself loving your partner deeply but feeling frustrated and hopeless due to constant arguments. You wish to return to the early days of your relationship, where your heart felt open, and vulnerability came naturally. Unfortunately, you might unintentionally place the blame on your partner for this shift in your emotional state.

This cycle often involves arguments followed by temporary reconnection, such as make-up sex, which can momentarily restore the feeling of openness and love. However, this cycle of fighting and reconciling only reinforces the pattern, leaving both partners feeling trapped and disconnected.

The intensity of arguments may escalate over time, with louder voices and harsher words, fuelled by the belief that you are not being understood or validated. As a result, physical symptoms like chest pain or tension in your body might arise, further straining your relationship. Feelings of resentment, exhaustion, and a desire for things to return to how they once were become prevalent.

To break this cycle and foster a deeply fulfilling relationship, it's crucial to focus on your own growth and self-improvement rather than expecting your partner to change. Understanding the root causes of your conflicts and working on personal transformation can significantly enhance both your relationship and overall well-being.

Journaling Prompts Based on Neuroscience to Heal Your Relationship:

- **Exploring Emotional Patterns:**
    - Reflect on the recurring patterns in your arguments. What emotions or triggers consistently arise during conflicts? How can recognising these patterns help in addressing the root causes?

- **Identifying Unresolved Feelings:**
  - Consider any unresolved feelings or past experiences that may be contributing to your current conflicts. How can addressing these underlying issues lead to more meaningful and less frequent arguments?

- **Understanding Vulnerability:**
  - Write about what vulnerability meant to you at the beginning of your relationship. How has your experience of vulnerability changed over time? What steps can you take to reintroduce this sense of openness?

- **Examining Conflict Triggers:**
  - List common triggers for conflicts between you and your partner. How do these triggers affect your emotional response? What strategies can you implement to manage these triggers more effectively?

- **Evaluating Communication Styles:**
  - Analyse your communication style during arguments. Are there specific ways you respond that escalate conflicts? How can you adjust your communication to foster a more understanding and empathetic dialogue?

- **Acknowledging Physical Symptoms:**
  - Reflect on any physical symptoms you experience during or after conflicts. How do these symptoms affect your emotional state and relationship? What can you do to alleviate these physical manifestations?

- **Reconnecting with Early Relationship Feelings:**
  - Write about the aspects of your early relationship that made you feel deeply connected and loved. How can you recreate or maintain these aspects in your current relationship?

- **Shifting Focus to Self-Improvement:**
  - Explore areas of personal growth that could positively impact your relationship. How can focusing on your own development enhance your ability to contribute to a healthier and happier partnership?

- **Creating a Vision for Change:**
  - Imagine your ideal relationship free from constant conflict. What specific changes would you need to make to achieve this vision? How can you work towards this ideal scenario?

- **Committing to Personal Transformation:**
  - Write about your commitment to improving yourself and opening your heart fully. What daily practices can support this commitment? How can focusing on your own growth positively influence your relationship?

By engaging with these prompts, you can gain clarity on the underlying issues contributing to your conflicts, develop strategies for personal growth, and create a more fulfilling and harmonious relationship.

Journaling Instructions

On the following pages, take the time to answer the questions from the journaling prompts provided in this chapter. These prompts are designed to help you reflect deeply on your relationship, uncover new insights, and foster greater understanding between you and your partner.

Use the journaling pages within this book to guide your reflections at the end of each chapter, and pair this with a separate notebook to journal twice daily. Morning journaling helps set your intentions, clarify your goals, and align your mindset for the day ahead. It activates the brain's prefrontal cortex, enhancing focus and decision-making. Evening journaling, on the other hand, allows for reflection on the day's experiences, processing emotions, and reinforcing positive neural pathways as you sleep.

By combining both practices, you're maximising the brain's ability to rewire itself toward emotional healing, self-awareness, and long-term well-being.

"The cycle of fighting and reconciling only feeds the pattern, leaving both partners feeling disconnected and trapped."

"True healing starts when we understand the root of our conflicts and take ownership of our personal growth."

"To break the cycle of conflict, shift your focus from blame to self-awareness, only then can you foster a fulfilling relationship."

Chapter 24

Exploring Emotional Patterns: *Reflect on the recurring patterns in your arguments. What emotions or triggers consistently arise during conflicts? How can recognising these patterns help in addressing the root causes?*

Chapter 25

Creating a Magical Relationship: Daily Practices for Lasting Love

To build a magical, fulfilling relationship, it's essential to recognise that both partners must actively and consistently contribute to its success. The relationship you have with yourself significantly impacts your connection with others, setting the tone for how you engage in your romantic partnership. By working on yourself first, you pave the way for a stronger, more vibrant relationship with your partner.

Creating a magical relationship requires daily effort, mutual care, and positive contribution. It's about nurturing a bond of trust, love, respect, admiration, and appreciation. Here's how to cultivate this kind of relationship:

1. Prioritise Daily Communication
Instead of spending your time on trivial activities like scrolling through your phone or watching TV, dedicate at least 30 minutes each day to a meaningful conversation with your partner. Regular communication is crucial for addressing unresolved issues and expressing thoughts and feelings. This practice strengthens your bond and deepens your love.

Journaling Prompt:
- Reflect on your daily communication with your partner. How can you ensure that these conversations are meaningful and fulfilling? What topics or feelings need more attention in your discussions?

2. Master the Art of Listening
Listening is a cornerstone of a strong relationship. Make it a priority to understand your partner's feelings, thoughts, and challenges without immediately offering advice. Practice active listening by letting your partner speak without interruption and asking if they need advice or just someone to listen.

Journaling Prompt:
- Assess your listening skills. Are there areas where you can improve? How can you better support your partner by being a more attentive listener?

3. Embrace Honesty and Openness

Being open and vulnerable is essential for building trust and a strong emotional connection. Strive to be approachable and receptive to feedback. Honesty fosters trust, while dishonesty can undermine it, causing confusion and distance between partners.

Journaling Prompt:
- Explore how honesty plays a role in your relationship. Are there areas where you or your partner may be struggling with openness? How can you foster a more honest and transparent dialogue?

4. Foster Empathy and Respect

Understanding and appreciating each other's feelings, attitudes, and values are crucial for a harmonious relationship. Cultivate empathy by recognising and validating your partner's emotions and perspectives.

Journaling Prompt:
- Reflect on how empathy and respect are present in your relationship. Are there moments where you or your partner could show more understanding? How can you actively practice empathy in your daily interactions?

Daily Rituals for a Magical Relationship
- **Daily Check-ins:**
  - Schedule a specific time each day for a heartfelt check-in with your partner. Use this time to discuss how each of you is feeling and any issues that need addressing.

- **Active Listening Sessions:**
  - Dedicate time each week to practice active listening. Ensure each partner has the opportunity to speak without interruptions and validate each other's feelings.

- **Honesty Hour:**
  - Set aside a regular time to discuss your thoughts and feelings honestly. Encourage transparency and address any concerns openly.

- **Empathy Exercises:**
  - Engage in activities that build empathy, such as discussing each other's dreams, challenges, and successes. Practice seeing things from your partner's perspective.

- **Appreciation Rituals:**
  - Create a habit of expressing gratitude and appreciation for each other daily. This could be through verbal affirmations, notes, or small gestures.

Journaling Prompts to Enhance Your Relationship:

- **Daily Communication:**
  - How did our daily conversation go today? What worked well, and what could be improved for tomorrow?

- **Listening Skills:**
  - Did I actively listen to my partner today? What are some ways I can enhance my listening skills?

- **Honesty and Openness:**
  - Were there any moments of dishonesty or hesitation today? How can I ensure that I maintain honesty and openness in our interactions?

- **Empathy and Respect:**
  - Reflect on a recent situation where empathy was needed. How did I respond, and how can I improve in showing respect and understanding?

- **Appreciation:**
  - What are three things I genuinely appreciate about my partner today? How can I express this appreciation effectively?

By integrating these practices and journaling prompts into your daily routine, you'll create a relationship filled with trust, love, and mutual respect. Start today, and watch as your relationship transforms into something truly magical.

Journaling Instructions

On the following pages, take the time to answer the questions from the journaling prompts provided in this chapter. These prompts are designed to help you reflect deeply on your relationship, uncover new insights, and foster greater understanding between you and your partner.

Use the journaling pages within this book to guide your reflections at the end of each chapter, and pair this with a separate notebook to journal twice daily. Morning journaling helps set your intentions, clarify your goals, and align your mindset for the day ahead. It activates the brain's prefrontal cortex, enhancing focus and decision-making. Evening journaling, on the other hand, allows for reflection on the day's experiences, processing emotions, and reinforcing positive neural pathways as you sleep.

By combining both practices, you're maximising the brain's ability to rewire itself toward emotional healing, self-awareness, and long-term well-being.

"The foundation of a magical relationship is built through daily communication, mutual care, and the choice to nurture love every day."

"True love isn't found, it's created, through consistent effort, trust, and an unwavering commitment to growing together."

Chapter 25

Reflect on your daily communication with your partner. How can you ensure that these conversations are meaningful and fulfilling? What topics or feelings need more attention in your discussions?

Chapter 26

The Art of Navigating Disagreements and Difficulties in Relationships

Building and maintaining a fulfilling relationship requires more than just love and attraction; it involves navigating through difficulties and disagreements with resilience and empathy. Throwing in the towel or retreating when faced with conflict is not a pathway to lasting happiness. Instead, embracing and working through these challenges with a willingness to face discomfort can lead to deeper understanding and connection.

Facing Discomfort with Compassion

When disagreements arise, they often stem from an inability to listen objectively. Subjective listening can make us feel personally attacked and prompt retaliatory responses that escalate conflicts. Recognising that both partners have the right to express their opinions, thoughts, and feelings without judgment is crucial.

Creating a safe space for open expression is essential. Here's how to approach these conversations effectively:

- **Request Uninterrupted Time:**
    - If you need to express something important, ask your partner for dedicated time to talk. You might say, "I'd like to have 10 minutes of your time to express how I feel, uninterrupted, for the benefit of our relationship." If immediate attention isn't possible, schedule a suitable time later in the day.

- **Frame Your Feelings with "I Feel":**
    - Start your sentences with "I feel" rather than "You make me." This helps avoid sounding accusatory and focuses on your emotions rather than blaming your partner. For example, instead of saying, "You make me feel ignored," try "I feel neglected when you spend hours watching TV and I'm left alone."

- **Communicate Needs Clearly:**
    - At the beginning of your conversation, request that your partner listens without interruption and saves comments for after you've finished. For instance, "I would appreciate it if you could listen for ten minutes without interrupting. I need to express my feelings for the benefit of our relationship."

Examples of Effective Communication

Here are examples of how to frame your feelings using "I feel":
- **Example 1:**
    - "I feel sad and neglected when you spend so much time watching TV and don't pay attention to me. I miss our connection and feel overlooked."

- **Example 2:**
    - "I feel hurt and unappreciated when you arrive late after making plans with friends, especially when I've gone through the effort to cook a special dinner."

- **Example 3:**
    - "I feel frustrated when I try to talk about something important, and it seems like you're not fully present or engaged in the conversation."

Journaling Prompts for Deepening Relationship Understanding
- **Reflect on Emotional Expression:**
    - How do I currently express my feelings during conflicts? Do I use "I feel" statements, or do I tend to blame my partner? How can I improve my communication?

- **Evaluate Listening Practices:**
    - When was the last time I listened to my partner without interruption? How did that affect our conversation? What can I do to be a better listener?

- **Identify Patterns in Disagreements:**
  - What are the common triggers for arguments in my relationship? How can I approach these triggers differently to reduce conflict?

- **Assess Emotional Safety:**
  - Do I feel that my partner and I create a safe space for each other to express feelings and opinions? How can we enhance this safety?

- **Examine Impact of Conflict Resolution:**
  - How does our current method of resolving disagreements affect our relationship? What changes can we make to ensure that conflicts lead to positive outcomes rather than increased tension?

By embracing these practices and using the journaling prompts, you can work towards a more harmonious relationship where both partners feel heard, understood, and valued. This approach helps transform conflicts into opportunities for growth, ultimately leading to a deeper, more fulfilling connection.

Journaling Instructions

On the following pages, take the time to answer the questions from the journaling prompts provided in this chapter. These prompts are designed to help you reflect deeply on your relationship, uncover new insights, and foster greater understanding between you and your partner.

Use the journaling pages within this book to guide your reflections at the end of each chapter, and pair this with a separate notebook to journal twice daily. Morning journaling helps set your intentions, clarify your goals, and align your mindset for the day ahead. It activates the brain's prefrontal cortex, enhancing focus and decision-making. Evening journaling, on the other hand, allows for reflection on the day's experiences, processing emotions, and reinforcing positive neural pathways as you sleep.

By combining both practices, you're maximising the brain's ability to rewire itself toward emotional healing, self-awareness, and long-term well-being.

Chapter 26

Reflect on Emotional Expression: *How do I currently express my feelings during conflicts? Do I use "I feel" statements, or do I tend to blame my partner? How can I improve my communication?*

Chapter 27

Cultivating Respectful Communication in Relationships

Effective communication is the cornerstone of any healthy and thriving relationship. It's crucial to avoid impulsive reactions like sending angry texts, screaming, or shouting at your partner. These actions can inflict emotional harm, leaving lasting scars that are difficult to heal. Instead, focus on expressing your feelings in person, in a manner that is respectful, compassionate, and rooted in love.

Guidelines for Expressing Feelings

- **Avoid Impulsive Reactions:**
  - Refrain from sending angry text messages or venting your frustrations through shouting. These actions can escalate the situation and cause more harm than good.
- **Express Feelings in Person:**
  - Wait until you are calm and can speak face-to-face with your partner. This allows for a more constructive and empathetic conversation.
- **Use "I Feel" Statements:**
  - Start your sentences with "I feel" rather than accusatory language. For example, "I feel hurt when..." rather than "You always..."

- **Distinguish Between Giving a 'Peace of Mind' and Expressing Feelings:**
  - Giving someone a "piece of your mind" is often about venting anger and frustration, which can damage the relationship. The goal should be to share your emotions in a way that helps both partners understand each other better, without inflicting pain.
- **Communicate with Respect and Compassion:**
  - Approach the conversation from a place of love. Your aim is to strengthen the relationship by being open and honest, not to hurt or demean your partner.

Journaling Prompts for Building Respectful Communication

1. **Reflect on Recent Conflicts:**
    - Think about the last argument you had with your partner. How did you express your feelings? Were there moments when you could have communicated more respectfully?
2. **Identify Triggers:**
    - What triggers you to react impulsively, such as sending an angry text or shouting? How can you recognise and manage these triggers better in the future?
3. **Practice Patience:**
    - Write about a time when you waited to express your feelings until you were calm. How did this impact the outcome of the conversation? How can you incorporate this patience into future interactions?
4. **Explore the Impact of Words:**
    - Consider a time when words from your partner hurt you deeply. How did it affect you? How can this understanding help you choose your words more carefully in your own communication?
5. **Plan for Future Conversations:**
    - Think of a situation that might upset you in the future. How can you prepare yourself to communicate your feelings calmly and effectively when it arises?

By implementing these strategies and reflecting on the journaling prompts, you can develop healthier communication habits that enhance your relationship. This approach fosters a deeper connection, mutual respect, and a stronger bond, paving the way for a more fulfilling partnership.

Journaling Instructions
On the following pages, take the time to answer the questions from the journaling prompts provided in this chapter. These prompts are designed to help you reflect deeply on your relationship, uncover new insights, and foster greater understanding between you and your partner.

Use the journaling pages within this book to guide your reflections at the end of each chapter, and pair this with a separate notebook to journal twice daily. Morning journaling helps set your intentions, clarify your goals, and align your mindset for the day ahead. It activates the brain's prefrontal cortex, enhancing focus and decision-making. Evening journaling, on the other hand, allows for reflection on the day's experiences, processing emotions, and reinforcing positive neural pathways as you sleep.

By combining both practices, you're maximising the brain's ability to rewire itself toward emotional healing, self-awareness, and long-term well-being.

"Speaking with kindness and clarity, even in disagreement, is the key to building lasting emotional safety in your relationship."

"Respectful communication turns conflict into connection, choosing words with care is an act of love."

Chapter 27

Reflect on Recent Conflicts: *Think about the last argument you had with your partner. How did you express your feelings? Were there moments when you could have communicated more respectfully?*

Chapter 28

Sustaining Love and Connection in Long-Term Relationships

In long-term relationships, it's easy to fall into a routine that can sometimes lead to complacency. However, greeting your partner with love and enthusiasm is a small but powerful way to maintain the warmth and connection that you shared at the beginning of your relationship.

Why Greetings Matter
When you greet your partner with genuine affection, a hug, a kiss, or even a heartfelt smile, you reinforce the bond that initially brought you together. This simple act communicates that you cherish and value your partner, and it sets a positive tone for your interactions. Neglecting this can make your partner feel taken for granted, which can gradually erode the intimacy and closeness in your relationship.

Guidelines for Loving Greetings
1. **Recreate the Early Connection:**
   - Recall how you greeted your partner when you first fell in love. Whether it was with a big hug, a passionate kiss, or simply the excitement in your voice, try to bring that same energy into your greetings now.
2. **Be Present:**
   - When your partner comes home, put away distractions like the TV or your phone. Stand up, make eye contact, and greet them warmly. This shows that you prioritise them and their presence in your life.
3. **Physical Touch:**
   - Incorporate a hug, a kiss, or even a gentle touch when you greet your partner. Physical touch is a powerful way to express love and build intimacy.
4. **Express Genuine Interest:**
   - After your initial greeting, ask about your partner's day with genuine interest. Listen actively, and let them know you care about what they have experienced.
5. **Consistency is Key:**
   - Make this a daily habit. Consistency in showing affection and attention helps keep the connection alive and prevents the relationship from becoming stale.

Journaling Prompts for Deepening Connection Through Greetings

1. **Reflect on Your Current Greeting Rituals:**
    - How do you typically greet your partner when they come home? Do you feel that your current greeting adequately expresses your love and appreciation? Why or why not?
2. **Remember the Early Days:**
    - Write about how you used to greet your partner in the early stages of your relationship. How did it make you feel? How did it make your partner feel? What has changed, and why?
3. **Visualise the Perfect Greeting:**
    - Imagine the ideal way you would greet your partner. What would you say? How would you touch them? How would this greeting make them feel? How would it make you feel?
4. **Identify Barriers:**
    - Are there any habits or distractions that prevent you from greeting your partner with love? What steps can you take to remove these barriers and prioritise your partner's presence?
5. **Plan to Improve:**
    - Write down specific actions you can take to improve how you greet your partner. How can you make them feel more loved and appreciated? Set an intention to practice these actions daily.

By consciously choosing to greet your partner with love and affection, you can sustain and even deepen the connection you share. These small, consistent efforts will contribute to a stronger, more fulfilling relationship over time.

Journaling Instructions
On the following pages, take the time to answer the questions from the journaling prompts provided in this chapter. These prompts are designed to help you reflect deeply on your relationship, uncover new insights, and foster greater understanding between you and your partner.

Use the journaling pages within this book to guide your reflections at the end of each chapter, and pair this with a separate notebook to journal twice daily. Morning journaling helps set your intentions, clarify your goals, and align your mindset for the day ahead. It activates the brain's prefrontal cortex, enhancing focus and decision-making. Evening journaling, on the other hand, allows for reflection on the day's experiences, processing emotions, and reinforcing positive neural pathways as you sleep.

By combining both practices, you're maximising the brain's ability to rewire itself toward emotional healing, self-awareness, and long-term well-being.

Chapter 28

Reflect on Your Current Greeting Rituals: *How do you typically greet your partner when they come home? Do you feel that your current greeting adequately expresses your love and appreciation? Why or why not?*

Chapter 29

Injecting Fun and Humour into Your Relationship

Just like air is essential for breathing, fun and humour are vital for the health of a relationship. While working on a relationship is important, it should never feel like a chore. Balancing effort with joy ensures that your bond remains strong and vibrant.

Why Fun and Humour Matter
Having fun together fosters intimacy and connection, helping couples build a reservoir of positive experiences that can be drawn upon during challenging times. Humour, particularly, can act as a pressure valve in tense moments, allowing couples to navigate disagreements or difficult situations with grace and goodwill. It lightens the mood, making it easier to handle life's inevitable ups and downs.

Incorporating Fun and Humour into Your Relationship
- **Make Time for Fun:**
  - **Plan Spontaneous Activities:** Surprise your partner with a spontaneous outing or activity. It could be something as simple as a picnic in the park, a hike, or a visit to a local museum. The key is to choose activities that both of you enjoy and that break the routine.
  - **Try New Things Together:** Keep your relationship exciting by exploring new hobbies or activities together. Whether it's trying a new recipe, attending a workshop, or learning a new sport, stepping out of your comfort zone together strengthens your bond.
  - **Weekly or Monthly Surprises:** Dedicate a day each week or month to surprise your partner with something fun. It doesn't have to be elaborate, sometimes, the best surprises are the simplest ones, like a homemade meal, a handwritten note, or an impromptu movie night.

- Cultivate a Sense of Humour:
  - **Laugh at Yourself:** Don't take yourself too seriously. Being able to laugh at your own mistakes or quirks not only lightens the atmosphere but also makes you more approachable and relatable to your partner.
  - **Tease Lightly and Playfully:** Light teasing and playful banter can add a fun dynamic to your relationship, as long as it's done with mutual respect and understanding. It helps to keep the mood light and reinforces the sense of camaraderie.
  - **Find Humour in Challenges:** When facing difficulties, try to see the lighter side of the situation. Humour can defuse tension and help you both maintain a positive perspective, making it easier to find solutions together.

- Keep the Spark Alive:
  - **Be Spontaneous:** Break away from routines now and then by doing something unexpected. Whether it's a spontaneous road trip, a surprise gift, or an unplanned date night, spontaneity keeps the relationship exciting and fresh.
  - **Create Inside Jokes:** Shared humour, especially inside jokes, can be a unique and intimate part of your relationship. These little moments of shared laughter build a deeper connection and create memories that are special to just the two of you.
  - **Plan for Playfulness:** Incorporate playful activities into your time together. It could be as simple as playing board games, having a dance-off in your living room, or engaging in a pillow fight. These moments of playfulness help to foster closeness and keep the relationship light-hearted.

Journaling Prompts to Enhance Fun and Humour

1. **Reflect on Fun Times:**
   - Think back to the last time you and your partner had a lot of fun together. What were you doing? How did it make you feel? How can you recreate similar moments regularly?
2. **List Fun Activities:**
   - Write down a list of activities that you both enjoy or have always wanted to try. How can you incorporate these activities into your relationship more often?
3. **Humor Inventory:**
   - Reflect on your sense of humour. How do you typically bring humour into your relationship? Are there ways you could be more playful or light-hearted with your partner?
4. **Plan a Surprise:**
   - Plan a fun surprise for your partner. What would make them smile or laugh? How can you execute this surprise in a way that shows thoughtfulness and care?
5. **Laugh Together:**
   - Think about the times when you and your partner laughed the hardest together. What triggered those moments? How can you encourage more of these light-hearted moments?

Conclusion

Integrating fun and humour into your relationship is not just about having a good time, it's about creating a lasting bond that can withstand life's challenges. By making an effort to keep things light, spontaneous, and joyful, you ensure that your relationship continues to grow and flourish. Remember, a couple that plays together, stays together!

Journaling Instructions
On the following pages, take the time to answer the questions from the journaling prompts provided in this chapter. These prompts are designed to help you reflect deeply on your relationship, uncover new insights, and foster greater understanding between you and your partner.

Use the journaling pages within this book to guide your reflections at the end of each chapter, and pair this with a separate notebook to journal twice daily. Morning journaling helps set your intentions, clarify your goals, and align your mindset for the day ahead. It activates the brain's prefrontal cortex, enhancing focus and decision-making. Evening journaling, on the other hand, allows for reflection on the day's experiences, processing emotions, and reinforcing positive neural pathways as you sleep.

By combining both practices, you're maximising the brain's ability to rewire itself toward emotional healing, self-awareness, and long-term well-being.

"Laughter is the heartbeat of a joyful relationship, fun and humour keep love light and full of life."

"Injecting fun into your relationship is like adding sunlight to a garden, it helps love grow and thrive."

Chapter 29

Reflect on Fun Times: *Think back to the last time you and your partner had a lot of fun together. What were you doing? How did it make you feel? How can you recreate similar moments regularly?*

Chapter 30

Never Stop Dating: Keep the Romance Alive

Maintaining a regular dating routine is crucial for keeping the romance alive in a relationship. Often, couples get caught up in the hustle and bustle of daily life, leading to neglecting this essential aspect of their relationship. However, regular dates can serve as a powerful way to reconnect, celebrate your love, and strengthen your bond.

Why Regular Dates Matter

1. **Reconnection:** Dating allows couples to step away from the routine and reconnect on a deeper level. It's a time to focus solely on each other, without the distractions of daily life.
2. **Celebration of Love:** Dates are special occasions to celebrate your relationship. They serve as a reminder of why you fell in love and what you appreciate about each other.
3. **Priority:** Regular dates signal to your partner that they are a priority in your life. It's an intentional way of showing that your relationship matters and deserves attention.

Tips for Successful Dates
- **Make It Regular:**
  - **Set a Schedule:** Decide on a frequency that works for both of you, whether it's weekly or fortnightly. Stick to this schedule as much as possible to create consistency.
  - **Vary the Experience:** Don't let your dates become routine. Mix things up by trying new restaurants, activities, or locations. This keeps the excitement alive.
- **Focus on Each Other:**
  - **No Phones:** Make a rule to keep phones away during dates. This ensures that you're fully present with each other, enhancing the quality of your time together.
  - **Engage in Conversation:** Use this time to engage in meaningful conversations. Ask open-ended questions, share your thoughts, dreams, and feelings, and truly listen to your partner.

- **Celebrate Your Relationship:**
  - **Express Appreciation:** During your dates, take time to express what you appreciate about your partner. Go beyond the surface and talk about the deeper qualities that you love and admire.
  - **Special Occasions:** Occasionally, elevate your date nights by planning something extra special, like a night in a hotel, a surprise dinner, or an activity you both love but don't do often.
- **Eliminate Arguments:**
  - **Prepare Mentally:** Before the date, remind yourself of the purpose, reconnection and celebration. Leave unresolved issues at home, or agree to discuss them at a different time, ensuring the date remains a positive experience.
  - **Focus on Positives:** Keep the conversation light and focus on positive aspects of your relationship. If a disagreement arises, handle it with kindness and a focus on resolution rather than conflict.
- **Incorporate Surprise:**
  - **Surprise Elements:** Occasionally, surprise your partner with an unexpected twist during your date. It could be a small gift, an unexpected activity, or simply a heartfelt note.
  - Be Spontaneous: While having a regular schedule is important, spontaneous dates can also add excitement

Journaling Prompts to Enhance Date Nights

- **Reflect on Past Dates:**
  - Think about the best dates you've had with your partner. What made them special? How can you recreate that magic in your future dates?
- **Plan Future Dates:**
  - Write down ideas for future dates. Consider what your partner enjoys and how you can make the experience meaningful and fun for both of you.
- **Express Appreciation:**
  - Before your next date, write down five things you appreciate about your partner. Use these thoughts as conversation starters during your date.

- **Resolve Issues:**
  - If there are recurring issues that come up during dates, reflect on how you can address them before the next outing. How can you create a positive atmosphere where both of you feel heard and appreciated?

- **Evaluate Your Effort:**
  - Consider how much effort you're putting into date nights. Are there ways you can be more creative or thoughtful in planning these times together?

Conclusion
Regular dating is not just an activity but a vital practice in maintaining and nurturing a healthy relationship. It's about prioritising each other, celebrating your love, and continuously finding new ways to connect. By committing to regular, meaningful dates, you ensure that your relationship remains vibrant, fulfilling, and full of love.

Journaling Instructions
Use the journaling pages within this book to guide your reflections at the end of each chapter, and pair this with a separate notebook to journal twice daily. Morning journaling helps set your intentions, clarify your goals, and align your mindset for the day ahead. It activates the brain's prefrontal cortex, enhancing focus and decision-making. Evening journaling, on the other hand, allows for reflection on the day's experiences, processing emotions, and reinforcing positive neural pathways as you sleep.

By combining both practices, you're maximising the brain's ability to rewire itself toward emotional healing, self-awareness, and long-term well-being.

"Regular dates are the heartbeat of lasting romance, a reminder that love thrives when it's nurtured with intention."

"In the hustle of life, regular dates are a sacred pause where love is prioritised and celebrated."

Chapter 30

Reflect on Past Dates: *Think about the best dates you've had with your partner. What made them special? How can you recreate that magic in your future dates?*

Chapter 31

Sharing Life Lessons: Fostering Growth Together

In any thriving relationship, continuous growth, both as individuals and as a couple, is essential. Sharing life lessons, personal insights, and experiences with your partner can be a powerful way to strengthen your connection and support each other's development. When you come across something that resonates with you, whether it's from a book, video, article, or personal experience, sharing it with your partner can create a deeper bond and mutual understanding.

Why Sharing Life Lessons Matters
1. **Encourages Mutual Growth:**
   - Sharing what you learn fosters an environment of continuous learning and growth within your relationship. It helps both partners to evolve together rather than apart.
2. **Builds Emotional Intimacy:**
   - Discussing meaningful insights and experiences can deepen your emotional connection, as it allows both partners to understand each other's perspectives, values, and personal journeys.
3. **Inspires Positive Change:**
   - When you share what has inspired or helped you, it can motivate your partner to reflect on their own life and possibly make positive changes that benefit both of you.
4. **Strengthens Communication:**
   - Regularly sharing life lessons encourages open and honest communication. It can lead to more meaningful conversations and a greater sense of partnership.

How to Share Life Lessons Effectively
- **Share Without Expecting Change:**
   - Approach the conversation with the intent to share your experience, not to change your partner. Focus on what resonated with you and why, without expecting your partner to adopt the same views or practices.

- **Be Vulnerable:**
  - When sharing, be open about your thoughts, feelings, and why the lesson or insight impacted you. Vulnerability can foster trust and deepen your connection.
- **Listen and Respect Their Perspective:**
  - After sharing, invite your partner to share their thoughts and feelings. Respect their perspective, even if it differs from yours, and be open to learning from their insights as well.
- **Keep It Positive:**
  - Frame the conversation in a positive light. Focus on what you've gained from the lesson, rather than what your partner should change. This encourages a supportive and non-judgmental exchange.
- **Make It a Two-Way Street:**
  - Encourage your partner to share their own life lessons and insights. This not only balances the exchange but also shows that you value their growth and experiences as much as your own.

Journaling Prompts to Enhance Life Lesson Sharing
1. **Reflect on Personal Growth:**
   - What is a recent life lesson or insight you've gained that has impacted you positively? How has it influenced your thoughts, feelings, or actions?
2. **Plan Your Sharing:**
   - How can you share this lesson with your partner in a way that is positive, non-judgmental, and encouraging? What are the key points you'd like to communicate?
3. **Anticipate Your Partner's Perspective:**
   - Consider how your partner might react to what you share. What questions or thoughts might they have? How can you be open to their perspective?
4. **Evaluate Your Intentions:**
   - Why do you want to share this lesson? Are you sharing to inspire, to connect, or to teach? Reflect on your motivations to ensure the sharing comes from a place of love and mutual growth.
5. **Follow-Up:**
   - After sharing, how did the conversation go? Did it lead to a deeper connection or new insights from your partner? What did you learn from the experience of sharing?

Conclusion

Sharing life lessons with your partner is a beautiful way to foster mutual growth, deepen your emotional connection, and build a strong foundation for your relationship. By approaching these conversations with openness, vulnerability, and respect, you create a space where both partners can learn from each other and grow together. This practice not only enhances your relationship but also contributes to your individual journeys towards self-improvement and fulfilment.

Journaling Instructions
On the following pages, take the time to answer the questions from the journaling prompts provided in this chapter. These prompts are designed to help you reflect deeply on your relationship, uncover new insights, and foster greater understanding between you and your partner.

Use the journaling pages within this book to guide your reflections at the end of each chapter, and pair this with a separate notebook to journal twice daily. Morning journaling helps set your intentions, clarify your goals, and align your mindset for the day ahead. It activates the brain's prefrontal cortex, enhancing focus and decision-making. Evening journaling, on the other hand, allows for reflection on the day's experiences, processing emotions, and reinforcing positive neural pathways as you sleep.

By combining both practices, you're maximising the brain's ability to rewire itself toward emotional healing, self-awareness, and long-term well-being.

"Growth together begins with sharing the lessons life teaches, transforming challenges into opportunities for deeper love."

"Sharing life lessons with your partner creates a bond rooted in growth, understanding, and mutual evolution."

Chapter 31

Reflect on Personal Growth: *What is a recent life lesson or insight you've gained that has impacted you positively? How has it influenced your thoughts, feelings, or actions?*

Chapter 32

Emotional Support and Compliments:
The Pillars of a Magical Relationship

In any thriving relationship, emotional support and genuine compliments play crucial roles in maintaining a deep and lasting connection. These elements not only reinforce love and respect but also create an environment where both partners feel valued, appreciated, and supported. By making a conscious effort to lift each other up and express appreciation daily, couples can nurture a bond that grows stronger over time.

The Importance of Emotional Support
1. **Building Trust and Safety:**
   - Emotional support fosters a sense of safety and trust in the relationship. When both partners feel secure knowing they can rely on each other for understanding and comfort, it deepens the bond between them.
2. **Encouraging Growth:**
   - Supportive partners encourage each other to pursue their goals and dreams. This mutual encouragement creates a dynamic where both individuals grow and evolve, benefiting the relationship as a whole.
3. **Enhancing Emotional Intimacy:**
   - Regular emotional support helps to build emotional intimacy, allowing both partners to share their vulnerabilities, fears, and hopes without fear of judgment.
4. **Reducing Stress:**
   - Life's challenges are easier to face when you know you have a supportive partner by your side. Emotional support acts as a buffer against stress, making it easier to navigate difficult times together.

The Power of Compliments
- **Fostering Appreciation:**
   - Compliments are a powerful way to show appreciation. They remind your partner that you notice and value their efforts, qualities, and presence in your life.

- **Boosting Self-Esteem:**
  - Genuine compliments can boost your partner's self-esteem and confidence. Knowing that their partner admires and appreciates them can help them feel better about themselves and their place in the relationship.
- **Strengthening Connection:**
  - Compliments that go beyond the surface, acknowledging deeper qualities and actions, strengthen the emotional connection between partners. They show that you see and value your partner for who they truly are.
- **Creating Positive Reinforcement:**
  - When you regularly compliment and appreciate your partner, it creates a positive reinforcement loop. This encourages both partners to continue contributing positively to the relationship.

Practical Ways to Give Emotional Support and Compliments
- **Daily Expressions of Gratitude:**
  - Make it a habit to express gratitude for your partner every day. Instead of just saying "I love you," try to be specific. For example, "I love how you always make me feel supported when I'm having a tough day."
- **Acknowledge the Small Things:**
  - Don't wait for grand gestures to give compliments. Acknowledge and appreciate the small things your partner does daily, such as making coffee in the morning or giving you a hug when you need it.
- **Compliment Their Character:**
  - Compliments that focus on your partner's character, like their kindness, resilience, or generosity, are particularly meaningful. These compliments go beyond superficial traits and show that you value who they are as a person.
- **Be a Cheerleader:**
  - Support your partner's goals and dreams by being their biggest cheerleader. Whether they're pursuing a career change, a new hobby, or personal development, your encouragement can make a huge difference.
- **Celebrate Achievements:**
  - Celebrate your partner's achievements, no matter how big or small. Let them know that you're proud of their hard work and accomplishments.

Journaling Prompts to Enhance Emotional Support and Compliments

1. **Reflect on Your Partner's Strengths:**
   - What are three qualities or strengths you admire most about your partner? How can you express your appreciation for these qualities in a way that will resonate with them?
2. **Identify Daily Acts of Support:**
   - What are some small but meaningful ways you can offer emotional support to your partner today? How can you be more attuned to their needs?
3. **Crafting Meaningful Compliments:**
   - Think about the last time your partner did something that made you feel loved or appreciated. How did it make you feel? Write down a compliment that you can share with them to express your gratitude.
4. **Plan a Praise Ritual:**
   - How can you incorporate daily or weekly praise into your relationship? Write down a plan for making this a regular practice, including specific times or situations where you will express your appreciation.
5. **Track Your Growth:**
   - Reflect on how regularly giving emotional support and compliments has impacted your relationship. What positive changes have you noticed? How can you continue to nurture this habit?

Conclusion

Emotional support and genuine compliments are essential for building and maintaining a magical relationship. By making these practices a daily habit, couples can create a relationship grounded in mutual respect, appreciation, and love. Through consistent effort and mindfulness, you can ensure that your partner feels valued and supported, leading to a deeper connection and a more fulfilling relationship.

Journaling Instructions

On the following pages, take the time to answer the questions from the journaling prompts provided in this chapter. These prompts are designed to help you reflect deeply on your relationship, uncover new insights, and foster greater understanding between you and your partner.

Use the journaling pages within this book to guide your reflections at the end of each chapter, and pair this with a separate notebook to journal twice daily. Morning journaling helps set your intentions, clarify your goals, and align your mindset for the day ahead. It activates the brain's prefrontal cortex, enhancing focus and decision-making. Evening journaling, on the other hand, allows for reflection on the day's experiences, processing emotions, and reinforcing positive neural pathways as you sleep.

By combining both practices, you're maximising the brain's ability to rewire itself toward emotional healing, self-awareness, and long-term well-being.

"A magical relationship thrives when both partners feel valued, appreciated, and unconditionally supported."

"Genuine compliments are more than words, they're affirmations of love that uplift and nurture your partner's soul."

Chapter 32

Reflect on Your Partner's Strengths: *What are three qualities or strengths you admire most about your partner? How can you express your appreciation for these qualities in a way that will resonate with them?*

Chapter 33

Love, Intimacy, Romance, and Sex: The Cornerstones of a Thriving Relationship

In any magical relationship, love, intimacy, romance, and sex are the essential elements that keep the connection between partners alive and vibrant. These aspects go beyond simply being together; they involve a continuous effort to deepen the bond, rekindle the spark, and ensure that both partners feel loved, desired, and appreciated. Here's how to nurture these cornerstones to maintain a thriving and magical relationship.

1. Love: The Foundation of Your Relationship
- **Consistent Acts of Love:**
    - Love in a relationship is shown through daily actions. These could be small gestures like making your partner's favourite coffee in the morning, leaving a sweet note, or simply being there to listen when they need to talk.
- **Expressing Love Verbally:**
    - Don't shy away from verbal expressions of love. Saying "I love you" should be a regular occurrence, but so should deeper expressions like, "I love how you make me feel safe" or "I love the way you always know how to make me smile."
- **Love Languages:**
    - Understand and speak each other's love languages. Whether it's words of affirmation, acts of service, receiving gifts, quality time, or physical touch, knowing how your partner prefers to give and receive love is crucial.

2. Intimacy: The Emotional Connection
- **Emotional Vulnerability:**
    - Intimacy begins with emotional vulnerability. Be open with your feelings, share your fears, dreams, and aspirations, and create a safe space for your partner to do the same. This deepens your connection and strengthens your emotional bond.

- **Shared Experiences:**
  - Build intimacy by sharing new experiences together. Whether it's trying a new hobby, traveling, or simply spending quality time together, these shared moments create lasting memories that bring you closer.
- **Physical Intimacy:**
  - Physical touch is a powerful way to maintain intimacy. Simple acts like holding hands, hugging, or cuddling can go a long way in making your partner feel loved and connected.

3. Romance: Keeping the Spark Alive
- **Plan Romantic Gestures:**
  - Romance doesn't have to be grand or expensive. Small, thoughtful gestures can keep the spark alive. Plan a surprise date, write a love letter, or prepare a candlelit dinner at home.
- **Celebrate Milestones:**
  - Celebrate your relationship milestones, no matter how small. Anniversaries, first dates, or even the day you first met are all opportunities to relive the romance and remind each other of your journey together.
- **Be Spontaneous:**
  - Keep the excitement alive by being spontaneous. Surprise your partner with a weekend getaway or an impromptu picnic. The element of surprise adds an exciting twist to your relationship.

4. Sex: The Physical Expression of Love
- **Open Communication:**
  - Talk openly about your sexual needs, desires, and boundaries. This ensures that both partners are on the same page and can work together to meet each other's needs.
- **Exploration and Experimentation:**
  - Don't be afraid to explore new things in the bedroom. Whether it's trying a new position, incorporating role-play, or using toys, keeping things fresh and exciting is key to a healthy sexual relationship.

- **Quality Over Quantity:**
  - Focus on the quality of your sexual encounters rather than the quantity. Make sure that each experience is satisfying and fulfilling for both partners, prioritising connection and pleasure.
- **Affection Outside the Bedroom:**
  - Maintaining physical affection outside of sex is crucial. Touching, kissing, and being physically close throughout the day helps keep the sexual connection strong.

Practical Tips to Enhance Love, Intimacy, Romance, and Sex

1. **Daily Affection:**
   - Make it a habit to show affection daily, whether it's through a kiss, a hug, or a kind word. These small acts build a foundation of love and intimacy.
2. **Regular Date Nights:**
   - Schedule regular date nights to keep the romance alive. Whether it's a fancy dinner out or a cozy night in, the key is to focus on each other and have fun.
3. **Communicate Your Desires:**
   - Be open about your desires and needs, both emotionally and physically. This honest communication is key to maintaining a healthy, fulfilling relationship.
4. **Surprise Your Partner:**
   - Every now and then, surprise your partner with a romantic gesture. It could be as simple as bringing them breakfast in bed or as elaborate as planning a surprise weekend away.
5. **Prioritise Intimacy:**
   - Make time for intimacy, both emotional and physical. Whether it's having a deep conversation, cuddling on the couch, or making love, these moments strengthen your bond.

Journaling Prompts to Enhance Love, Intimacy, Romance, and Sex

1. **Reflect on Your Love Language:**
   - What is your love language, and what is your partner's? How can you incorporate more of your partner's love language into your daily interactions?
2. **Exploring Emotional Intimacy:**
   - Write about a time when you felt deeply connected to your partner emotionally. What made that moment special? How can you create more of these moments?
3. **Planning a Romantic Gesture:**
   - What's one romantic gesture you can plan for your partner this week? How will you execute it, and how do you think it will make them feel?
4. **Discussing Sexual Desires:**
   - Reflect on your sexual relationship. Are there any desires or fantasies you haven't shared with your partner? How can you bring them up in a way that feels comfortable?
5. **Keeping the Spark Alive:**
   - What are some ways you can keep the spark alive in your relationship? List three things you can do this month to add excitement to your love life.

Conclusion

Maintaining a magical relationship requires continuous effort in the areas of love, intimacy, romance, and sex. By being intentional in these aspects, couples can keep their connection strong, their love vibrant, and their relationship fulfilling. With open communication, regular affection, and a commitment to nurturing the relationship, the spark can be rekindled and sustained, leading to a truly thriving and magical partnership.

Journaling Instructions

On the following pages, take the time to answer the questions from the journaling prompts provided in this chapter. These prompts are designed to help you reflect deeply on your relationship, uncover new insights, and foster greater understanding between you and your partner.

Use the journaling pages within this book to guide your reflections at the end of each chapter, and pair this with a separate notebook to journal twice daily. Morning journaling helps set your intentions, clarify your goals, and align your mindset for the day ahead. It activates the brain's prefrontal cortex, enhancing focus and decision-making. Evening journaling, on the other hand, allows for reflection on the day's experiences, processing emotions, and reinforcing positive neural pathways as you sleep.

By combining both practices, you're maximising the brain's ability to rewire itself toward emotional healing, self-awareness, and long-term well-being.

"Love is the foundation, but intimacy, romance, and passion are the sparks that keep the fire of a relationship alive."

"A thriving relationship is built on love expressed through moments of affection, whispered words of desire, and a mutual commitment to passion."

"When love, intimacy, romance, and sex come together, they create a magical harmony that sustains and enriches a relationship over time."

Chapter 33

Reflect on Your Love Language: *What is your love language, and what is your partner's? How can you incorporate more of your partner's love language into your daily interactions?*

Chapter 34

Sharing Goals and Dreams: Building a Future Together

In a thriving relationship, partners not only support each other's individual aspirations but also work together towards shared goals and dreams. This mutual support fosters a sense of unity and purpose, helping both individuals grow personally and as a couple. Here's how to navigate the balance between personal and mutual goals to create a fulfilling and harmonious partnership.

1. Understanding and Supporting Individual Goals
- **Respecting Personal Aspirations:**
  - Each partner should have their own set of goals and dreams. These may relate to career ambitions, personal growth, hobbies, or health. Respecting and encouraging your partner's individual goals shows that you value their personal development and happiness.
- **Providing Emotional and Practical Support:**
  - Be your partner's biggest cheerleader. Whether it's offering words of encouragement, helping with planning, or simply being there when they need to talk, your support can make a significant difference in their journey towards achieving their goals.
- **Balancing Time and Effort:**
  - While pursuing individual goals, it's important to balance time and effort so that your relationship doesn't take a backseat. Make sure that the pursuit of personal aspirations doesn't lead to neglecting your partner or your relationship.

2. Creating and Pursuing Mutual Goals
- **Identifying Shared Dreams**:
  - Sit down together and discuss what you both want to achieve as a couple. These could include buying a home, traveling to certain destinations, starting a family, or even small goals like learning a new skill together. Identifying shared dreams gives you something to look forward to as a team.
- **Setting Clear Goals:**
  - Once you've identified mutual goals, break them down into clear, actionable steps. Whether it's saving money for a big purchase or planning a trip, having a roadmap makes the journey towards these goals more manageable and enjoyable.

- **Regular Check-ins:**
  - Regularly discuss your progress towards mutual goals. This not only keeps you both on track but also strengthens your bond as you work together towards something meaningful.

3. Maintaining Respect and Sensitivity
- **Healthy Communication:**
  - Open and respectful communication is key when discussing goals and dreams. Make sure both partners feel heard and valued, and avoid dismissing each other's aspirations, even if they differ from your own.
- **Avoiding Manipulation or Control:**
  - Respect each other's boundaries and avoid using manipulative or controlling tactics to influence your partner's goals. A healthy relationship is built on mutual respect, not coercion.
- **Supporting Autonomy:**
  - While it's important to have mutual goals, it's equally vital to allow each other the autonomy to pursue individual aspirations. Encouraging each other's personal growth ultimately benefits the relationship as a whole.

4. Building a Future Together
- **Long-Term Vision:**
  - Develop a shared vision for your future. Discuss where you see yourselves in five, ten, or even twenty years. This could include everything from career plans and family life to where you want to live and how you want to spend your retirement.
- **Flexibility and Adaptability:**
  - Life is unpredictable, and sometimes goals may need to change. Be flexible and adaptable, and be willing to adjust your plans as needed. What's most important is that you navigate these changes together.
- **Celebrating Milestones:**
  - As you achieve your mutual goals, take the time to celebrate these milestones. Whether big or small, these celebrations reinforce your commitment to each other and the future you're building together.

Journaling Prompts to Support Goal-Setting in Relationships

1. **Reflect on Individual Goals:**
   - What are your top three personal goals, and why are they important to you? How can your partner support you in achieving them?
2. **Identify Mutual Goals:**
   - What are some goals you and your partner share? How can you work together to achieve these goals, and what steps will you take first?
3. **Communication Check-In:**
   - How do you currently communicate about goals and dreams with your partner? What could you improve in your communication to ensure both of you feel heard and supported?
4. **Balancing Personal and Mutual Aspirations:**
   - Reflect on the balance between your personal goals and your shared goals. Are you dedicating enough time and effort to both? If not, how can you better balance these priorities?
5. **Vision for the Future:**
   - What does your ideal future together look like? Write down a vision for your relationship in five years. What mutual goals will you have achieved, and what personal growth will you have experienced?

Conclusion

Sharing goals and dreams is a vital aspect of a thriving relationship. By supporting each other's individual aspirations and working together towards mutual goals, couples can build a future that is both fulfilling and aligned with their shared vision. Open communication, mutual respect, and a commitment to each other's growth will ensure that both partners feel valued and supported in their journey together. With the right balance and a clear roadmap, you can create a partnership that is both successful and deeply satisfying.

Journaling Instructions

On the following pages, take the time to answer the questions from the journaling prompts provided in this chapter. These prompts are designed to help you reflect deeply on your relationship, uncover new insights, and foster greater understanding between you and your partner.

Use the journaling pages within this book to guide your reflections at the end of each chapter, and pair this with a separate notebook to journal twice daily. Morning journaling helps set your intentions, clarify your goals, and align your mindset for the day ahead. It activates the brain's prefrontal cortex, enhancing focus and decision-making. Evening journaling, on the other hand, allows for reflection on the day's experiences, processing emotions, and reinforcing positive neural pathways as you sleep.

By combining both practices, you're maximising the brain's ability to rewire itself toward emotional healing, self-awareness, and long-term well-being.

"A relationship blossoms when partners champion each other's aspirations and create a joint roadmap that leads to success and lasting joy."

"When partners unite their individual goals with mutual dreams, they create a future rich with purpose, love, and fulfilment."

Chapter 34

Reflect on Individual Goals: *What are your top three personal goals, and why are they important to you? How can your partner support you in achieving them?*

_____

_____

_____

_____

_____

_____

_____

_____

_____

_____

_____

_____

_____

_____

Chapter 35

Compassion, Acceptance, and Forgiveness: Navigating Difficult Times Together

Every relationship faces challenges, some of which may be beyond your control. During these times, the strength of your relationship is tested, and your ability to practice compassion, acceptance, and forgiveness becomes crucial. These qualities are the pillars that will help you and your partner weather the storms of life together, emerging stronger and more connected.

1. Practicing Compassion
- **Understanding and Empathy:**
  - Compassion begins with empathy, putting yourself in your partner's shoes and understanding their feelings and experiences. When your partner is going through a tough time, be patient and offer them the emotional support they need. This might involve listening without judgment, offering a comforting presence, or simply being there for them in whatever way they need.
- **Offering Emotional Support:**
  - Emotional support is about being a steady source of comfort for your partner. This could mean offering words of encouragement, holding them during difficult moments, or just sitting in silence together. Compassionate support shows your partner that they are not alone, and that you are there for them unconditionally.
- **Responding with Kindness:**
  - During stressful situations, it's easy to react with frustration or anger. Instead, strive to respond with kindness. This means being gentle with your words and actions, even when emotions are running high. Kindness in communication can prevent misunderstandings and help you both feel more connected and understood.

2. Embracing Acceptance
- **Acknowledging Differences:**
  - No two people are exactly alike, and differences in opinions, behaviours, and reactions are natural in any relationship. Acceptance involves recognising and embracing these differences without trying to change your partner. It's about loving them for who they are, not who you want them to be.

- **Letting Go of Control:**
  - Sometimes, situations arise that you cannot control or fix. Acceptance means letting go of the need to control every aspect of your relationship and understanding that some things are beyond your influence. This can help reduce stress and create a more peaceful, harmonious relationship.
- **Respecting Boundaries:**
  - Acceptance also involves respecting your partner's personal boundaries, including their emotional and physical space. This respect fosters a sense of safety and trust in the relationship, allowing both partners to feel secure and valued.

3. Practicing Forgiveness
- **Healing Through Forgiveness:**
  - Forgiveness is essential in any long-term relationship. Holding onto grudges or past hurts can create a rift between partners and erode the foundation of trust. Forgiveness doesn't mean forgetting or condoning hurtful behaviour; it means letting go of resentment and choosing to move forward with a clean slate.
- **Communicating Forgiveness:**
  - When offering forgiveness, communicate openly with your partner about how you feel. Discuss what happened, why it hurt, and how you both can work to prevent similar issues in the future. Clear communication helps both partners understand each other's perspectives and fosters healing.
- **Self-Forgiveness:**
  - Forgiveness isn't just about forgiving your partner, it's also about forgiving yourself. We all make mistakes, and holding onto guilt or self-blame can be damaging. Practice self-compassion and recognise that personal growth often involves learning from mistakes.

4. Navigating Difficult Times Together
- **Emotional Resilience:**
  - Resilience is the ability to bounce back from adversity. In a relationship, this means supporting each other through difficult times, maintaining hope, and finding strength in your connection. Resilient couples view challenges as opportunities to grow together rather than as threats to their relationship.

- **Objective Perspective:**
  - When faced with a challenge, try to look at the situation objectively. Instead of reacting emotionally, take a step back and assess the issue calmly. Discuss the problem with your partner, focusing on finding solutions rather than assigning blame.
- **Weathering the Storms:**
  - Difficult times are inevitable, but how you handle them together defines the strength of your relationship. Approach challenges as a team, with the understanding that you are in this together. This united front not only helps you overcome obstacles but also deepens your bond.

Journaling Prompts to Cultivate Compassion, Acceptance, and Forgiveness

1. **Reflect on Compassion:**
   - Think of a recent situation where your partner needed support. How did you respond, and how could you have shown more compassion? What steps can you take to be more understanding and supportive in the future?
2. **Acceptance in Your Relationship:**
   - What are some differences between you and your partner that you've found challenging to accept? How can you work towards embracing these differences and finding value in them?
3. **Forgiveness Process:**
   - Recall a time when you had to forgive your partner or yourself. What was the experience like, and how did it impact your relationship? What can you learn from this to improve your approach to forgiveness in the future?
4. **Building Resilience:**
   - How do you and your partner typically handle difficult situations? What strategies could you both implement to strengthen your emotional resilience and navigate challenges more effectively together?
5. **Communicating During Tough Times:**
   - Reflect on how you communicate with your partner during difficult times. Are there ways you can improve your communication to ensure it is more compassionate, accepting, and forgiving?

Conclusion

Compassion, acceptance, and forgiveness are the cornerstones of a resilient and thriving relationship. By practicing these qualities, you create a safe and supportive environment where both partners feel valued, understood, and loved. Navigating life's challenges together with kindness and empathy not only strengthens your bond but also ensures that your relationship remains a source of comfort and joy, no matter what obstacles you face. Embrace these practices, and watch your relationship grow deeper and more fulfilling with each passing day.

Journaling Instructions

On the following pages, take the time to answer the questions from the journaling prompts provided in this chapter. These prompts are designed to help you reflect deeply on your relationship, uncover new insights, and foster greater understanding between you and your partner.

Use the journaling pages within this book to guide your reflections at the end of each chapter, and pair this with a separate notebook to journal twice daily. Morning journaling helps set your intentions, clarify your goals, and align your mindset for the day ahead. It activates the brain's prefrontal cortex, enhancing focus and decision-making. Evening journaling, on the other hand, allows for reflection on the day's experiences, processing emotions, and reinforcing positive neural pathways as you sleep.

By combining both practices, you're maximising the brain's ability to rewire itself toward emotional healing, self-awareness, and long-term well-being.

"A relationship thrives not because it avoids challenges, but because both partners choose compassion and empathy over judgment and blame."

"The real strength of a relationship lies in practicing acceptance and compassion, ensuring that both partners feel valued, loved, and understood through life's trials."

Chapter 35

Reflect on Compassion: *Think of a recent situation where your partner needed support. How did you respond, and how could you have shown more compassion? What steps can you take to be more understanding and supportive in the future?*

Chapter 36

Embracing a Mutual Desire to Step Outside the Box: Expanding Horizons Together

In any relationship, falling into routines and patterns is natural, but it can also lead to stagnation. To keep the relationship vibrant and growing, it's essential to cultivate a mutual desire to explore new ideas, experiences, and perspectives. This willingness to "step outside the box" together fosters a deeper connection, encourages personal and relational growth, and helps overcome challenges rooted in past experiences.

1. The Value of Stepping Outside the Box
- **Breaking Away from Routine:**
  - Routine can be comforting, but it can also lead to complacency. By consciously choosing to break away from the usual patterns and trying something new, you inject excitement and novelty into your relationship. This could be as simple as trying a new hobby together, exploring a new place, or even learning something new as a couple.
- **Challenging Old Beliefs:**
  - Each partner enters a relationship with a set of beliefs, shaped by past experiences. These beliefs, while valid, can sometimes hinder growth. Being open to questioning and challenging these beliefs allows both partners to grow individually and as a couple. This openness can lead to a more profound understanding and appreciation of each other.
- **Shared Growth:**
  - Couples who learn and grow together build a stronger bond. Whether it's taking a class, attending workshops, or reading books on relationship improvement, the shared experience of learning fosters a sense of unity and common purpose. It also equips both partners with new tools and perspectives to navigate challenges.

2. Overcoming the Influence of the Past
- **Identifying Past Influences:**
  - Past experiences can heavily influence present relationships, often in ways that aren't immediately obvious. Reflecting on how past hurts, traumas, or learned behaviours might be affecting your current relationship is the first step toward overcoming these challenges.
- **Communicating About the Past:**
  - Open communication about past experiences is crucial. Sharing your past with your partner, including your fears, hurts, and learned behaviours, allows both of you to understand each other better. This understanding can lead to greater empathy and a stronger connection.
- **Creating New Patterns:**
  - Once you've identified how the past might be influencing your present, work together to create new, healthier patterns. This might involve setting new boundaries, developing new communication strategies, or simply being more mindful of how the past shapes your reactions and behaviours.

3. Exploring New Ideas and Experiences Together
- **Learning New Skills:**
  - Take on the challenge of learning something new together. This could be anything from a cooking class, learning a new language, or even taking up a new sport. The process of learning together not only brings you closer but also adds a sense of adventure and accomplishment to your relationship.
- **Travel and Exploration:**
  - Travel is a great way to step outside the box. Exploring new places and cultures together can open your minds to new perspectives and create lasting memories. Even local travel, such as weekend getaways or day trips to nearby towns, can offer new experiences and a break from routine.
- **Trying New Relationship Strategies:**
  - Don't be afraid to experiment with new strategies to enhance your relationship. This might include trying new ways of communicating, introducing regular date nights, or even exploring different forms of intimacy. The key is to keep things fresh and engaging.

4. Facing Challenges Together
- **Developing a Growth Mindset:**
  - Adopting a growth mindset as a couple means being open to change, learning, and improvement. Instead of seeing challenges as obstacles, view them as opportunities to grow and strengthen your relationship. This mindset encourages both partners to continually seek ways to enhance their connection.
- **Supporting Each Other's Growth:**
  - It's important to support each other in individual growth as well. Encourage your partner to pursue their interests, learn new skills, or explore new ideas, even if it means stepping outside of their comfort zone. This support fosters mutual respect and appreciation.
- **Thinking Creatively:**
  - When facing difficulties, think creatively about how to address them. Instead of relying on old patterns or solutions, brainstorm new ways to resolve issues. This might involve seeking outside help, such as counselling or coaching, or simply trying a different approach to problem-solving.

Journaling Prompts to Foster a Mutual Desire to Step Outside the Box

1. **Reflect on Routine:**
   - What routines have you and your partner fallen into that might be leading to complacency? How can you break away from these routines and introduce more novelty and excitement into your relationship?
2. **Challenge Old Beliefs:**
   - What beliefs or patterns from your past might be influencing your current relationship? How can you work with your partner to challenge and change these beliefs for the better?
3. **Explore New Experiences:**
   - What new experiences or activities could you and your partner explore together? How can these new experiences strengthen your bond?
4. **Addressing Past Influences:**
   - How have past experiences shaped your current relationship? What steps can you take as a couple to address any negative influences from the past?
5. **Creativity in Problem-Solving:**
   - Think of a recent challenge you and your partner faced. How could you have approached it more creatively? What new strategies can you try in the future to address challenges together?

Conclusion
Stepping outside the box in a relationship is about more than just trying new activities, it's about being open to growth, challenging old patterns, and exploring new possibilities together. By fostering a mutual desire to learn, grow, and experience life in new ways, you not only keep your relationship fresh and exciting but also build a deeper, more resilient bond. Embrace the adventure of stepping outside the box together, and watch your relationship thrive in ways you never thought possible.

Journaling Instructions
On the following pages, take the time to answer the questions from the journaling prompts provided in this chapter. These prompts are designed to help you reflect deeply on your relationship, uncover new insights, and foster greater understanding between you and your partner.

Use the journaling pages within this book to guide your reflections at the end of each chapter, and pair this with a separate notebook to journal twice daily. Morning journaling helps set your intentions, clarify your goals, and align your mindset for the day ahead. It activates the brain's prefrontal cortex, enhancing focus and decision-making. Evening journaling, on the other hand, allows for reflection on the day's experiences, processing emotions, and reinforcing positive neural pathways as you sleep.

By combining both practices, you're maximising the brain's ability to rewire itself toward emotional healing, self-awareness, and long-term well-being.

Chapter 36

Reflect on Routine: *What routines have you and your partner fallen into that might be leading to complacency? How can you break away from these routines and introduce more novelty and excitement into your relationship?*

Chapter 37

Admitting Mistakes and Communicating Effectively in Relationships

In any relationship, mistakes are inevitable. The key to maintaining a strong and healthy connection lies in how you handle these mistakes, both your own and those of your partner. Admitting mistakes and addressing them with kindness and compassion, rather than defensiveness or anger, can transform conflicts into opportunities for growth and deeper understanding.

1. The Importance of Admitting Mistakes
- **Personal Growth:**
    - Admitting mistakes is an essential part of personal growth. It requires humility and self-awareness. When you acknowledge your errors, you demonstrate that you are willing to learn and improve, which fosters trust and respect in the relationship.
- **Modeling Integrity:**
    - By admitting your mistakes, you set a positive example for your partner. This modelling of integrity encourages them to do the same, leading to a healthier, more open relationship.
- **Reducing Conflict:**
    - Addressing mistakes directly and openly reduces the likelihood of resentment and frustration building up. It prevents small issues from escalating into major conflicts.

2. Communicating About Mistakes
- **Use "I Feel" Statements:**
    - When discussing mistakes, use "I feel" statements to express your emotions without assigning blame. For example, "I feel upset when we miss our flight because I was looking forward to our trip," rather than "You always mess things up."
- **Practice Active Listening:**
    - Active listening involves fully concentrating on what your partner is saying, understanding their perspective, and responding thoughtfully. This practice helps ensure that both partners feel heard and respected.

- **Avoid Defensiveness:**
  - When your partner points out a mistake, resist the urge to become defensive. Instead, listen to their concerns and discuss the issue calmly. Defensiveness can escalate conflicts and prevent constructive dialogue.

3. Strategies for Effective Communication
- **Acknowledge Mistakes Promptly:**
  - When you realise you've made a mistake, address it as soon as possible. This shows responsibility and a willingness to rectify the situation.
- **Use Empathy:**
  - Try to understand how your partner feels about the situation. Empathising with their experience helps in addressing the issue more compassionately.
- **Apologize Sincerely:**
  - A genuine apology involves acknowledging the mistake, expressing regret, and making amends if necessary. A sincere apology can diffuse tension and rebuild trust.
- **Seek Solutions Together:**
  - Focus on finding solutions rather than dwelling on the mistake. Collaborate with your partner to prevent similar issues in the future.

4. Journaling Prompts for Effective Communication and Handling Mistakes
- **Reflect on Recent Mistakes:**
  - Think about a recent mistake you made. How did you address it? How did your partner respond? What could you have done differently to handle the situation better?
- **Analyse Your Reactions:**
  - When your partner makes a mistake, how do you typically react? Do you tend to become defensive or do you approach the situation with understanding? How can you improve your reactions?
- **Explore Feelings of Mistakes:**
  - Reflect on a situation where a mistake caused you emotional discomfort. How did you express your feelings? How did your partner respond? What would you like to change in your communication?

- **Empathy in Mistakes:**
    - Recall a time when your partner admitted a mistake. How did you respond? Did you show empathy and understanding? How can you enhance your empathy in future situations?
- **Creating Positive Communication Habits:**
    - What are some positive communication habits you can implement when discussing mistakes? How can you incorporate "I feel" statements and active listening into your daily interactions?
- **Developing Solutions Together:**
    - Reflect on a past conflict caused by a mistake. What steps did you take to resolve it? How can you involve your partner more effectively in finding solutions?

5. **Building Integrity and Consistency**
- **Align Words and Actions:**
    - Ensure that your actions align with your words. Integrity in communication builds trust and reinforces your commitment to the relationship.
- **Consistency in Behavior:**
    - Maintain consistency in how you address mistakes and communicate with your partner. Consistent behaviour fosters stability and reliability in the relationship.
- **Commit to Growth:**
    - Continuously work on improving your communication skills and handling mistakes constructively. Personal and relational growth is an ongoing process.

Conclusion

Admitting mistakes and addressing them with kindness, compassion, and effective communication is crucial for a thriving relationship. By focusing on personal growth, practicing active listening, and using empathy, you can turn challenges into opportunities for deeper connection and understanding. Embrace the journey of growth together, and your relationship will become more resilient, fulfilling, and joyful.

> If you must choose between being kind or being right,
> always choose kind,
> and you will always be right.
> Dr Wayne Dyer

Journaling Instructions

On the following pages, take the time to answer the questions from the journaling prompts provided in this chapter. These prompts are designed to help you reflect deeply on your relationship, uncover new insights, and foster greater understanding between you and your partner.

Use the journaling pages within this book to guide your reflections at the end of each chapter, and pair this with a separate notebook to journal twice daily. Morning journaling helps set your intentions, clarify your goals, and align your mindset for the day ahead. It activates the brain's prefrontal cortex, enhancing focus and decision-making. Evening journaling, on the other hand, allows for reflection on the day's experiences, processing emotions, and reinforcing positive neural pathways as you sleep.

By combining both practices, you're maximising the brain's ability to rewire itself toward emotional healing, self-awareness, and long-term well-being.

"The path to a thriving relationship is paved with honest admissions and compassionate dialogue, where each mistake becomes a lesson in love and understanding."

Chapter 37

Reflect on Recent Mistakes: *Think about a recent mistake you made. How did you address it? How did your partner respond? What could you have done differently to handle the situation better?*

Chapter 38

Discussing Taboo Topics to Deepen Your Relationship

Exploring and discussing taboo topics in a relationship can lead to greater intimacy and understanding. Addressing these subjects openly and honestly can help partners connect on a deeper level, resolve conflicts, and strengthen their bond. Here's a guide to approaching these discussions, along with journaling prompts based on neuroscience to enhance your relationship.

1. Finance
- **Why It's Important:**
    - Money can be a significant source of stress and conflict in relationships. Discussing finances openly ensures that both partners are on the same page regarding spending, saving, and financial goals.
- **Discussion Tips:**
    - Share your financial goals and worries.
    - Discuss budgeting, saving strategies, and any debt management plans.
    - Address how money affects your relationship and lifestyle choices.
- **Journaling Prompts:**
    - What are my financial goals, and how do they align with my partner's goals?
    - How do I feel about our current financial situation? What changes would I like to see?
    - How do financial stressors impact our relationship, and how can we address them?

2. Job/Business
- Why It's Important:
    - Career satisfaction and job stress can affect your relationship. Understanding each other's work-related challenges and achievements fosters empathy and support.
- **Discussion Tips:**
    - Share your job satisfaction and any professional challenges.
    - Discuss how work impacts your personal life and relationship.
    - Explore career goals and how they align with your life plans.

- **Journaling Prompts:**
  - What are my career aspirations, and how do they fit into our life together?
  - How does my job affect my mood and our relationship?
  - What support do I need from my partner regarding my career?

3. Love & Intimacy
- **Why It's Important:**
  - Love and intimacy are core components of a thriving relationship. Discussing your needs, desires, and any issues in this area promotes a deeper connection.
- **Discussion Tips:**
  - Talk about what intimacy means to each of you.
  - Share your desires and any changes you'd like to see in your intimate life.
  - Address any concerns or issues openly.
- **Journaling Prompts:**
  - What do I need from my partner to feel loved and fulfilled?
  - How do I express love and intimacy, and how does my partner receive it?
  - What are my desires and expectations regarding intimacy?

4. Giving and Contributing
- **Why It's Important:**
  - Mutual contribution strengthens the relationship. Discuss how each of you can contribute to the relationship in meaningful ways.
- **Discussion Tips:**
  - Share how you'd like to contribute to the relationship and household.
  - Discuss how you can support each other in daily life and long-term goals.
  - Address any imbalances in contributions.
- **Journaling Prompts:**
  - How do I currently contribute to our relationship and household?
  - What more could I do to support my partner?
  - How can we ensure a balanced contribution from both sides?

5. **Learning**
   - **Why It's Important:**
     - Continuous learning and personal growth are vital for a fulfilling relationship. Discuss your interests and goals for learning and development.
   - **Discussion Tips:**
     - Share what you're currently learning or interested in.
     - Explore how you can support each other's learning goals.
     - Discuss any new skills or hobbies you'd like to pursue together.
   - **Journaling Prompts:**
     - What are my current interests and learning goals?
     - How can my partner support my learning and growth?
     - What new experiences would I like to explore with my partner?

6. **Communication**
   - **Why It's Important:**
     - Effective communication is crucial for resolving conflicts and building a strong relationship. Discuss how you can improve your communication skills.
   - **Discussion Tips:**
     - Talk about your communication styles and any issues you've encountered.
     - Discuss how you can better understand each other's needs and perspectives.
     - Explore strategies for more effective and empathetic communication.
   - **Journaling Prompts:**
     - How do I currently communicate with my partner, and what could I improve?
     - What are the main communication issues we face, and how can we address them?
     - How can we create a more open and supportive communication environment?

7. **Home**
   - **Why It's Important:**
     - Your home environment impacts your relationship and daily life. Discuss how you want to manage and enjoy your living space together.

- **Discussion Tips:**
  - Share your vision for your home environment and any changes you'd like.
  - Discuss responsibilities for home maintenance and decoration.
  - Explore ways to create a comfortable and enjoyable living space.
- **Journaling Prompts:**
  - What do I envision for our home, and how does that align with my partner's vision?
  - How can we improve our living environment to better suit both of us?
  - What are the responsibilities I'd like to share in maintaining our home?

8. Family
- **Why It's Important:**
  - Family dynamics can significantly affect your relationship. Discuss your roles and boundaries regarding family interactions.
- **Discussion Tips:**
  - Share your thoughts on family involvement and boundaries.
  - Discuss how you want to handle family events and issues.
  - Explore any concerns or expectations regarding family interactions.
- **Journaling Prompts:**
  - What are my expectations regarding family involvement in our lives?
  - How do family dynamics affect our relationship?
  - What boundaries or changes would I like to establish with our families?

9. Goals, Values, and Motivation
- **Why It's Important:**
  - Shared goals and values provide direction and unity. Discuss your individual and mutual goals and how they align with your values.
- **Discussion Tips:**
  - Talk about your personal and joint goals.
  - Explore how your values align and any differences.
  - Discuss how you can support each other in achieving your goals.

- **Journaling Prompts:**
  - What are my personal and shared goals, and how do they align with my values?
  - How can I support my partner in achieving their goals?
  - What motivates me, and how can we use that motivation in our relationship?

10. Household Chores
- **Why It's Important:**
  - Fair distribution of household chores can prevent resentment and ensure a harmonious home environment. Discuss how chores are divided and managed.
- **Discussion Tips:**
  - Share your expectations for household responsibilities.
  - Discuss how to fairly divide chores and responsibilities.
  - Explore any issues or frustrations related to household tasks.
- **Journaling Prompts:**
  - How do I feel about the current division of household chores?
  - What changes would I like to see in managing household responsibilities?
  - How can we improve our approach to handling chores together?

11. Health & Sickness
- **Why It's Important:**
  - Health issues can impact both partners and the relationship. Discuss how you can support each other's health and manage sickness together.
- **Discussion Tips:**
  - Share your health concerns and any needs related to sickness or wellness.
  - Discuss how you can support each other in maintaining health.
  - Explore how to handle health crises and long-term health issues.
- **Journaling Prompts:**
  - What are my health concerns, and how can my partner support me?
  - How do we handle sickness and health issues as a couple?
  - What steps can we take to improve our overall health and wellness together?

12. Confidentiality
- **Why It's Important:**
  - Maintaining confidentiality builds trust and ensures that personal information is handled respectfully. Discuss boundaries regarding privacy and sharing information.
- **Discussion Tips:**
  - Share your expectations for handling confidential information.
  - Discuss how you'll manage sensitive topics and privacy.
  - Explore any concerns about sharing personal information.
- **Journaling Prompts:**
  - How do I define confidentiality in our relationship?
  - What are my concerns regarding privacy and sharing information?
  - How can we ensure we respect each other's confidentiality and privacy?
  -

13. Fidelity
- **Why It's Important:**
  - Fidelity is crucial for trust and security in a relationship. Discuss your expectations and boundaries regarding fidelity and commitment.
- **Discussion Tips:**
  - Share your views on fidelity and what it means to each of you.
  - Discuss any concerns or expectations about commitment and exclusivity.
  - Explore how you can strengthen your bond and commitment.
- **Journaling Prompts:**
  - What does fidelity mean to me, and how does it impact our relationship?
  - How do I feel about our level of commitment and exclusivity?
  - What actions can we take to reinforce our commitment to each other?

14. Feelings & Emotions
- **Why It's Important:**
  - Understanding and validating each other's feelings and emotions promotes empathy and connection. Discuss how you handle emotions and support each other.

- **Discussion Tips:**
  - Share how you feel about different aspects of your relationship.
  - Discuss how you handle and express emotions.
  - Explore how you can better support each other emotionally.
- **Journaling Prompts:**
  - How do I express my feelings and emotions in our relationship?
  - How can my partner better support me emotionally?
  - What changes can we make to improve our emotional connection?

15. Friendship
- **Why It's Important:**
  - Friendship within a relationship strengthens the bond and creates a supportive and enjoyable partnership. Discuss how you can cultivate and maintain your friendship.
- **Discussion Tips:**
  - Share what friendship means to you in the context of your relationship.
  - Discuss ways to strengthen your friendship and enjoy each other's company.
  - Explore any areas where you'd like to improve your connection and support.
- **Journaling Prompts:**
  - What does friendship mean to me in our relationship?
  - How can we improve our friendship and connection?
  - What activities or habits can we adopt to strengthen our bond?

Conclusion
Discussing taboo topics openly and honestly helps to deepen your understanding of each other and strengthens your relationship. Regularly exploring these areas, using the journaling prompts, and creating a safe space for these conversations can lead to a more fulfilling and resilient partnership. Embrace the opportunity to connect on a deeper level and continually nurture your relationship.

Chapter 38

What are my financial goals, and how do they align with my partner's goals? How do I feel about our current financial situation? What changes would I like to see? How do financial stressors impact our relationship, and how can we address them?

Chapter 39

Building a Relationship Foundation: Insights from My Journey

In the early stages of my relationship with my wife, Nadia, we knew that marriage was in our future. Just three months in, we recognised the importance of understanding each other deeply, especially on topics often considered taboo. We took the proactive step of drafting a relationship agreement, spending an entire weekend discussing our thoughts and feelings on crucial aspects of life and partnership.

Key Areas We Covered:
- **Finance:** We discussed our financial philosophies, how we would manage money, and set mutual financial goals.
- **Love and Intimacy:** We explored what love and intimacy mean to each of us, ensuring that we were aligned in our expectations and desires.
- **Giving and Contributing:** We agreed on how we would contribute to our relationship and household, striving for a balanced and supportive partnership.
- **Communication:** We committed to open, honest communication, addressing how we would handle conflicts and misunderstandings.
- **Home and Family:** We shared our visions for our home and family life, ensuring that we were on the same page about future plans.
- **Goals and Values:** We identified our personal and mutual goals, discussing how our values would guide our decisions and actions.
- **Health and Sickness:** We talked about how we would support each other in times of illness, and how we could maintain our health together.
- **Confidentiality and Fidelity:** We established clear boundaries around trust, privacy, and commitment, ensuring that our relationship was built on a foundation of faithfulness and respect.

Creating a Relationship Manifesto: We also developed a relationship manifesto, a living document that we agreed to amend as our relationship evolved. This manifesto outlined our commitments to each other, the principles we would live by, and how we would handle potential challenges in the future.

As our relationship grew, we continued to learn and implement new strategies to contribute positively to our partnership. This constant growth and learning have been the key to our happiness and the deep love we share.

The Power of Consistency and Commitment
By the time we celebrated our seventh wedding anniversary in August 2024, our relationship had blossomed into something truly magical. With a beautiful 3-year-old son, our love continues to grow stronger and more enchanting each day. We are showered with unconditional love and happiness, and not a day goes by without feeling immense gratitude for the life and family we've built together.
This profound connection, rooted in joy and deep affection, is what I aim to share with others through this book, my workshops, and seminars. My mission is to teach people worldwide how to cultivate and sustain the same unconditional love, happiness, and magical relationships in their own lives.

Just as we need to breathe to survive, our relationship needed constant nurturing to flourish. We made a conscious effort to keep our love fresh and our bond strong, always looking for ways to contribute more positively as a couple.

Practical Application: A 90-Day Challenge
Before considering giving up on your relationship, I encourage you to take on a 90-day challenge. The principles and exercises outlined in this book, when practiced for ninety consecutive days, can lead to profound healing of past traumas and significant improvements, not only in your relationship but also in how you view yourself. Through this process, you'll cultivate deeper self-love, greater happiness, and an expanded capacity to love unconditionally. These 90 days are about transformation at the core, helping you rewire emotional patterns and bring your best self into the relationship.

This challenge is not just about making efforts to improve your relationship, but about working on yourself. It's about showing up every day with a mindset of contributing selflessly and unconditionally. By committing to this process, you're giving your relationship the space to thrive and evolve beyond the ordinary.

In my experience as a coach, I've witnessed remarkable transformations in clients who fully embrace this challenge. After ninety days of consistent effort, they report feeling deeper love, genuine happiness, and a renewed sense of fulfilment in their relationships, stronger than ever before. This transformation is available to anyone willing to commit wholeheartedly.

Journaling Prompts to Guide Your Journey:
1. **Reflect on the Beginning:**
   - What drew you to your partner initially? How have those qualities evolved over time?
   - How did you feel during your early conversations about taboo topics?
2. **Assess Your Current Relationship:**
   - In what areas do you feel your relationship has grown the most?
   - Are there any areas where you feel stuck or need more growth?
3. **Vision for the Future:**
   - What new goals or aspirations do you want to set for your relationship?
   - How can you continue to contribute positively to your relationship in the coming years?
4. **Self-Reflection:**
   - How have you grown personally since the beginning of your relationship?
   - What habits or practices have helped you maintain and strengthen your relationship?
5. **Challenge Yourself:**
   - What specific actions will you take during the next 90 days to improve your relationship?
   - How will you measure the success of your efforts?

To improve your relationship over the next 90 days, it's essential to engage in a structured approach with specific actions, tools for progress tracking, and measurable outcomes. Here's a step-by-step guide on what actions to take and how to evaluate success:

To improve your relationship over the next 90 days, it's essential to engage in a structured approach with specific actions, tools for progress tracking, and measurable outcomes. Here's a step-by-step guide on what actions to take and how to evaluate success:

Specific Actions for Improvement
- **Daily Intentional Gratitude:** Every day, write down three things you genuinely appreciate about your partner. Express these to them verbally, which will foster positive communication and reinforce emotional connection.
- **Active Listening Practice:** Dedicate time each day for uninterrupted conversations where the focus is solely on understanding your partner's thoughts and feelings, rather than responding or reacting. This builds trust and mutual respect.
- **Conflict Resolution Techniques:** Use the "I feel" communication technique rather than accusatory language. When conflict arises, focus on sharing emotions without blame, promoting a healthier, non-defensive dynamic.
- **Weekly Check-ins:** Set aside time every week to reflect on the state of your relationship. Discuss what's working well and where improvements can be made in a calm, constructive manner.
- **Quality Time Commitment:** Schedule at least one date night or bonding activity each week. Make it a time to connect without distractions, deepening emotional intimacy.
- **Daily Affection Rituals:** Incorporate acts of physical affection like hugs, kisses, and gentle touches every day. Neuroscience shows that these simple acts release oxytocin, strengthening emotional bonds.
- **Mindfulness or Meditation Together:** Engage in mindfulness exercises or guided meditations to centre yourselves individually and as a couple. This practice helps calm emotional reactivity and enhances self-awareness.

Tools to Measure and Evaluate Progress
- **Journaling:** Keep a relationship journal to track daily gratitude, emotions, and interactions. Journaling helps to measure your emotional state, identify triggers for conflict, and note moments of connection. Use this to reflect on changes in emotional dynamics over time.

- **Partner Feedback:** At the end of each week, ask your partner how they feel the relationship is progressing. Use specific, open-ended questions like "How connected do you feel this week?" or "What areas do you think we could improve on?"
- **Mood and Emotion Tracking:** Use mood-tracking apps or keep a personal log of your emotional highs and lows each day. Over time, you should see fewer instances of negative emotions such as frustration or anger.
- **Relationship Satisfaction Survey:** Create a simple survey where you both rate aspects of the relationship on a scale of 1 to 10, communication, intimacy, conflict resolution, trust, and overall happiness. Do this once a month to gauge progress.
- **Behavioural Changes:** Track changes in behaviours like reducing negative habits (e.g., criticising, defensiveness) and increasing positive behaviours (e.g., showing affection, expressing gratitude). Notice how frequently arguments arise and whether they are becoming less frequent or more manageable.
- **Calendar of Commitments:** Use a shared digital calendar to schedule weekly check-ins, date nights, or mindfulness sessions. Ensure that you are both consistently showing up for these activities as a measure of commitment.
- **End-of-Day Reflection:** At the end of each day, ask yourself, "Did I contribute positively to the relationship today?" Use this as a personal accountability tool to measure how aligned your actions are with the goals of the 90-day challenge.

How Will You Measure Success?

Success in the 90-day challenge can be measured through several key indicators:

- **Improved Emotional Connection:** Fewer arguments, more open conversations, and a stronger sense of intimacy indicate that emotional barriers are breaking down.
- **Increased Trust:** Both partners feel secure and trusted, with less need for reassurance or control behaviours like checking each other's phones.
- **Enhanced Relationship Satisfaction:** As measured through weekly feedback, both partners feel happier and more fulfilled.
- **Consistency in Positive Actions:** Your ability to maintain daily positive habits (gratitude, affection, quality time) shows commitment to the process.

- **Conflict Resolution:** If conflicts still arise, they should be handled with more patience, understanding, and mutual respect, indicating emotional growth.
- **Personal Well-being:** You'll notice improvements in your personal happiness and self-love, as this challenge not only transforms the relationship but also your internal state.

By consistently applying these strategies and measuring progress using these tools, you'll gain a clear picture of how both you and your relationship are evolving over the 90 days.

Conclusion
A magical relationship requires effort, consistency, and a willingness to grow together. By tackling taboo topics, creating a relationship manifesto, and committing to ongoing self-improvement, you can achieve profound relationship bliss. Take on the 90-day challenge, and you may find that your relationship transforms in ways you never thought possible.

Journaling Instructions
On the following pages, take the time to answer the questions from the journaling prompts provided in this chapter. These prompts are designed to help you reflect deeply on your relationship, uncover new insights, and foster greater understanding between you and your partner.

Use the journaling pages within this book to guide your reflections at the end of each chapter, and pair this with a separate notebook to journal twice daily. Morning journaling helps set your intentions, clarify your goals, and align your mindset for the day ahead. It activates the brain's prefrontal cortex, enhancing focus and decision-making. Evening journaling, on the other hand, allows for reflection on the day's experiences, processing emotions, and reinforcing positive neural pathways as you sleep.
By combining both practices, you're maximising the brain's ability to rewire itself toward emotional healing, self-awareness, and long-term well-being.

> "In a truly magical relationship, love isn't something you chase or grasp at; it's something you nurture from within. The more you cultivate self-love and emotional resilience, the more you radiate love that attracts a relationship full of profound connection and joy."

Chapter 39

Reflect on the Beginning: *What drew you to your partner initially? How have those qualities evolved over time? How did you feel during your early conversations about taboo topics?*

A 90-Day Challenge

The 90-Day Challenge serves as a powerful conclusion to The Love Reset, bringing together the core principles of the book to inspire deep transformation. This challenge is designed to create lasting change in your life, your relationships, and your sense of self-worth by committing to daily reading, journaling, and applying the techniques provided for 90 consecutive days.

The Science Behind the 90-Day Challenge
Neuroscience tells us that consistent practice and reinforcement over time are key to rewiring the brain. Through the concept of neuroplasticity, your brain has the ability to form new, healthier neural pathways. By engaging in daily journaling and mindful exercises, you're actively reshaping your brain's wiring, helping you heal from past traumas, build self-love, and improve emotional resilience. Over 90 days, these repeated efforts can lead to profound changes in how you think, feel, and engage in your relationships.

Benefits of the 90-Day Challenge
- **Healing Emotional Trauma:** Daily reflection helps bring unresolved issues to the surface, allowing you to face them head-on and release their emotional grip on you. The book provides guided exercises to help you process these emotions, so by the end of the challenge, you're not only more aware of your emotional triggers but are also equipped with tools to manage them.
- **Building Self-Love:** By dedicating time each day to reflect and nurture yourself through self-care practices, you're learning to prioritise your own well-being. Self-love is essential in building healthy relationships. This challenge encourages the use of daily affirmations, gratitude exercises, and self-compassion techniques to strengthen your sense of self-worth.
- **Improving Relationships:** As you grow emotionally and mentally, you'll find that your relationships also begin to transform. The principles from The Love Reset focus on creating stronger, healthier bonds by shifting your mindset away from attachment towards true love. This daily work encourages greater communication, empathy, and understanding between partners.

- **Measurable Progress:** Journaling not only allows you to express your thoughts and feelings but also gives you a record of your growth. Over the 90 days, you can look back at your entries and see how your mindset has shifted, how past emotional wounds have begun to heal, and how your relationships have improved.

Practical Tools for Success

To ensure success in your 90-Day Challenge, follow these actionable steps:
- **Daily Journaling:** Commit to writing at least once a day, preferably twice, once in the morning and again at bedtime. Use the prompts provided at the end of each chapter or your own reflections to explore your emotional state, goals, and progress.
- **Daily Reading:** Set aside time each day to read a passage from the book. This keeps you aligned with the techniques and exercises that you need to implement, ensuring that the lessons stay fresh in your mind.
- **Evaluating Progress:** At the end of each week, review your journal to measure your emotional progress. Track improvements in your self-esteem, how you handle conflicts, and your overall sense of happiness. Ask yourself: How am I growing? How is my relationship changing?
- **Support System:** If possible, share your journey with a trusted friend or therapist. Discussing your experiences adds an extra layer of accountability and support as you go through the challenge.

Conclusion: Transformation Through Consistency
By fully committing to the 90-Day Challenge, you'll be investing in a future where trauma no longer dictates your emotional reactions, self-love is central to your daily life, and your relationships thrive on a foundation of mutual respect and trust. The small, consistent efforts you make each day will lead to profound transformation not just in your love life, but in every area of your existence. Embrace the journey, and let The Love Reset guide you towards the life and relationships you deserve.

More About the Author: Eldin Hasa
Eldin Hasa is a distinguished neuroscientist with over 18 years of experience, renowned for his deep expertise in human behaviour. As the author of the influential book *Are We All F*cked?*, Eldin explores the complexities of the human mind, offering profound insights into how our thoughts, emotions, and behaviours shape our lives. His work has resonated globally, establishing him as a leading authority in personal development and mental well-being.

In addition to his writing, Eldin is a sought-after coach for elite and ultra-high-net-worth (UHNW) individuals, providing personalised guidance that empowers his clients to reach their highest potential. His unique approach, grounded in neuroscience, has made him the go-to expert for those seeking to enhance their performance, resilience, and overall quality of life.

Eldin's impact extends to the corporate world, where he serves as a top-tier trainer and speaker. His corporate training programs are celebrated for their transformative effects, helping organisations optimise leadership, communication, and team dynamics. With a focus on applying the latest research in neuroscience to real-world challenges, Eldin equips companies with the tools they need maintain and sustain change, and to thrive in a competitive environment.

As the host of the acclaimed podcast *The Human Experience*, Eldin delves into a wide array of topics, from human behaviour and mental health to business strategy and societal trends.
Through engaging conversations with thought leaders, experts, and influencers, he provides his audience with valuable perspectives on how to navigate the complexities of modern life.

Eldin's expertise has been widely recognised by the media. He has been featured in leading publications such as *The Mirror, Metro, Daily Mail, iNews, Ladbible, Women's Health, Yahoo*, and has appeared on *BBC radio and TV*. His ability to translate complex scientific concepts into practical advice has earned him a reputation as a trusted voice in both the academic and public spheres.

With a career dedicated to exploring the depths of human potential, Eldin Hasa continues to inspire and empower individuals and organisations around the world. His work is a testament to the power of understanding the human mind and using that knowledge to lead a more fulfilling, purposeful life.

"Through daily journaling and practising the techniques in this book, you'll heal old wounds, rediscover your self-worth, and create the life and love you've always deserved."

"Daily self-love practices from The Love Reset are like brushing your heart clean, removing the buildup of trauma and negativity, making room for happiness and healthy relationships."

Notes

Notes

Notes

Printed in Great Britain
by Amazon

67098c35-aadd-4e62-b35d-7a9c7938a26fR01